I0680439

BALTIC MIST

A Timeless Saga

BALTIC MIST

A Timeless Saga

Book One

By Jennifer Lohr

Copyright © Jennifer Lohr, An Ancient

Approach, 2013   All rights reserved

Except for brief quotations in review, this

book or any parts thereof may not be reproduced

in any form, without permission of the copyright

owner.

An Ancient Approach – 2014

ISBN 978-0-61593-442-6

I dedicate this book series, in its entirety, to the woman behind the real Helga Thorfinsdotter. Without you there simply would have been no inspiration to tell this tale. Whoever you are…thank you.

Book 1 – Contents

Acknowledgments

I cannot express enough thanks for the editing services provided by Norse Mythologist Dr. Karl E.H. Seigfried. Without your help this project could not have been completed, and I am humbled to have had the privilege of working with you.

Thanks to my four babies who had to share me with my computer while I finished my "work." You inspire me to be the very best I can be, and I wouldn't want to be anyone else than your mommy!

Last but not least, special thanks to my husband Scott, my biggest fan. Your caring and loving support carried me along the long hours needed to make this a success. Thanks for all your help with the house, among other things. The whole experience brought us closer. I love you madly.

Preface

Many people hold stories within – little tales locked in a vault in their minds, and they are able to remember them. Some go on to write these stories down…much like I did here.

…Then how could you write a book about Vikings? How is this your *story?* One might ask.

To answer that, I should explain that my protagonist Helga is not an original character. She was first mentioned in *Egil's Saga*, an Icelandic saga written over one thousand years ago. Seeing a blank canvas in the young woman, I began my tale with her.

In completing this project, I have come to the conclusion that many of us are unaware of the enormous influence the age-old

Scandinavian culture and Norse Mythology / Paganism still has today, even in our predominantly Christian, western / modern societies.

I was simply compelled to tell this story, and shed light on these ancient and fascinating people.

Introduction

It may surprise you to know that, despite the subject matter, this is not a fantasy novel series.

I quite enjoy the many fantasy titles available, and am not judging any of them, *or* their talented creators; but to be clear, it's imperative you are informed that although I obviously hope to keep you entertained, there *is* a hidden agenda: to introduce what life may have been like for a holy woman, living in the Viking age.

Throughout the series, I did my utmost to remain historically correct where possible, while retaining a sense of realism. I hope to convey a relatable human experience, viewed from the perspective of a viable member of her society, and as she may have seen the world.

Many portions of this book series were derived from sagas themselves such as <u>Egil's Saga</u> and the <u>Völuspá Saga</u>, as well as the many scholarly studies of them and other saga literature.

In July 2013, <u>Science News</u> published the findings of Pádraig Mac Carron and Ralph Kenna, after the pair gathered data from 18 different sagas (including Egil's Saga) and a network of 1,549 characters. They wanted to test if the stories were just fiction, or based on real society – their conclusion? "Remarkably realistic."

Hoping to stay as culturally and religiously correct as possible, I also utilized Jenny Jochens' <u>Women in Old Norse Society</u>, and Rudolf Simek's <u>Dictionary of Northern Mythology</u>, thanks to the suggestion from my editing support.

Lastly, you might be surprised to find the substantial role women in archaic Scandinavian society had – one that I am disappointed to find missing in the many modern Viking and /or Scandinavian motion pictures, and literature.

Recalling the Oseberg ship burial of Norway, dated to 834 AD, a long ship and its contents were perfectly preserved in the massive undertaking to honor the death of two völvas, or Norse prophetesses.

Additionally, it should be mentioned the great influence these women had upon the Scandinavian people. Evidence of this was documented as early as 58 BCE by Julius Caesar, when he wrote of discord between his troops under Ariovistus against Germanic tribesmen. He described Germanic women dressed in white who sacrificed the prisoners of war and sprinkled their blood in order to prophesy coming events, and advised war strategy each morning prior to battle.

Finally, on the island of Sweden's Birka, among the many graves unearthed within the last three centuries, one was noted as being the final resting place for a Völva and a warrior, buried together. Above them, a spear was positioned.

Some theorized it was done in dedication to Odin

and Freyja.

CHAPTER ONE

Journey home with me

My name is *Mist,* and know it was your fate, decided ages ago, to hear my tale. I am a legend whose legacy *you* are now part of, as you join me in history. Know as you read this: all is as it should be, for there are no accidents. Destiny has brought you and I together, our connection has finally been made. This day was once foreseen, and your time to know me has come. Although I breathed in the air centuries before as

19

you do now, pieces of me continue on. Come, as I now wish to show you not who I *was*, but rather *who I am*....

Follow me back to my time, before the likes of all that you know now, here and today. Visit alongside me my beloved northern homeland as it once was, so very long ago. Behold its massive forests – so lush, green, and already ancient by the time of my existence. Come to where great cascading rivers spill over rocky cliffs, where their spray can be felt, splashing on the rolling hills below.

The dawning of my life was a special time for my parents. I would be their firstborn maid-child. I took my first breaths during the period after the Yule Festival and before the coming of spring, when the earth gave way to a warmer sun and seeds of growth. After my birth it was told my mother, Hilde, accepted me by permitting me to nurse milk from her breast. It was then my father tearfully held me on his knee and passionately announced,

"It is known, a daughter has been born: Helga Thorfinsdotter…she belongs to me, Thorfinn Bondesson. I choose her name in honor of my mother, who is now among the dead." He then sprinkled drops of water over my tiny infant body.

This was the way I became a member of my family, officially, and they rejoiced in the goddesses Frigg and Freyja. Many were grateful to the two goddesses for delivering me safely from my mother's womb, while leaving her unscathed and in good health, for I was brought forth humbly, with the assistance of only a single helping-woman when typically two were needed. Mother bore me at our home in the region of Eida Skog, within the immense forest at the heart of Norway.

Soon after, my mother's belly brought upon our household another blessing of a child. This birth was that of a boy-child. He healthily suckled and grew past the age of concern where, sadly, many an infant did not thrive beyond. He was named Helgi, and grew to be a strong, fearless young man.   His bravery matched warriors twice his age, and he lived true to the laws of the land. Helgi was a fine addition to complement the pride found in our honorable name.

My parents' marriage was not the typical wedded arrangement of our time. Hilde's parents hadn't the chance to follow through in their own agreement; sadly, they succumbed to a terrible illness – one which she and her brothers thankfully survived.   After their parents were gone, the hardship of managing their sheep farm was very difficult for Hilde's brothers; and they decided against marrying her off. They guarded her interests of any wedding negotiations, in replacement of their father.

Two men very suitable to wed had been turned down by her brothers. It became apparent to Hilde their indecision was not the reason for the refusals, but rather their reluctance to become short-handed. Legally, she was permitted to accept the third proposal from Thorfinn's family, and she did.

After the feasting of the celebration, she joined Thorfinn in Eida Skog. Accompanied by her rightful portion of sheep from her family's farm, she began her new role as woman of the house. This was the way we Norse lived. Ownership of livestock, land, and other assets over-ruled love, a factor absent in the conditions of a marriage.

Hilde often stated I would follow her lineage of women-folk, all of whom were versed in the distinctive and specialized gift of *seiðr* – the ability to *see* things that others could not, and *know* truths unspoken to most. Hilde herself was acclaimed as a well-known prophetess, known to my people as a *völva*.

Since mother was versed in the art of seiðr, she frequently traveled to assist others with her skill. With her wand as her companion, she donned an elaborate cloak – hooded, lined with fur, and ornamented with jeweled pieces. Its blue shade held special meaning, symbolizing death; but such reference did not indicate evil, but rather the wisdom held by these *seeing* women. It was believed by my people much knowledge could be gained from those who had passed on into the realm of the dead, just as our god Odin did, when he desired to learn of his future. He rose up from death a very wise völva so ancient, she was older than the giants that once walked the earth and was present at the very beginning of creation. She explained to him how all came to be.

"You, too, will practice as a völva one day, daughter. Know of the lineage from which you come, since my mother and her clan of mothers before are of the goddess Frigg. This is where my power of prophecy comes from, little Helga." She first told me when I was a small child, only three years of age, in her usual confident tone.

"*When* will I see, mother?" My tiny voice asked her as I squinted my eyes, to better concentrate and focus. Mother looked down at me, smiling.

"You will know when, Helga. It will be when the moment is right for you." She held my chin and kissed my nose, as she affectionately sometimes did when I was a child. We then would return to working the enormous loom in our hall, so I may continue with my part in weaving as she began to sing. Mother had such a glorious voice, and the beauty in which she expressed her *Varðlokur* would leave me in awe. Hilde was an expert in such rhymes. Although she typically sang them during her rituals or ceremonies, she would also sing them to me, softly and gently.

Thorfinn, my sovereign, uncomplicated, and sensible father, took much pride in being a bondi – unrestrained by affluence or royalty. He was great-grandson of a thrall – a slave of another. Tales passed down told that his forefather redeemed himself by granting his

27

owner full payment. He compensated not only for himself, but his entire family's freedom. This great feat had many reasons to it, but most importantly so he may raise his children *free*. In generations, property was also obtained with, not only money, but with alliances made. Neighboring families swore to each other in life, blood, and death.

Being the quiet and hard-working man he was, father was also intelligent and of sound mind. Even as every calloused finger on father's rough hands were crooked from bone breaks, his skin remained dry and cracked, and his feet sat covered in sores... it was his heart that was content, leaving his soul pure. True, my family needn't work the land we lived on by our hands alone, but the level of dignity gained by such an accomplishment meant more to Thorfinn. Over the course of time, no amount of paid servants could ever substitute the harmony and pride he held within.

Once I was of age, Thorfinn was adamant I would marry the son of Erik, a nearby farmer, in hopes a spoiled confederation could be renewed. The only reason for this merging was a simple one: to make amends, legally.

"When it is time, daughter, you will be given to Hendrik. Our families will finally and lawfully be at peace. All will know this by your marriage, child." He taught me as early as I can remember, the importance in the planned unity – for it would affect generations to come, all beginning with Hendrik and I.

As farmers, husbandry was our primary objective, and in view of this our cattle were of great value. So much was their worth, we attributed the same word for cows, bulls, and calves as we did for money: '*fé.*'

Thorfinn's father and Erik's father had a dispute many years before in regards to some cattle grazing along the boundary of their adjacent fields. Each man insisted the other held his rightful beasts, and all relations halted. The conflict carried on, affecting the homes of both families – and to an extreme degree of hatred. This was all until Thorfinn and Erik grew old enough to head households of their own. The two men had always held a liking for one another; and it was friendship rather than rivalry they found, since they were both children. However, the discord overshadowed the adolescent boys' comradery, and they dared not tell of their own closeness.

How Thorfinn and Erik both roared in hilarity as they caroused with each other, while drinking mead and remembering the amusement in their sport of disguised capers. The pair could hardly contain their laughter when they told of how their own mothers' old house-maidens equally deduced, "it must be one of the hidden folk," whom each boy went off to frolic with. Each of us present in their company could not help but join in on their merriment, as we all listened to their entertaining tales.

Often enough as they ended another enjoyable encounter, the two men would bid each other a favorable night, always with father holding his own face. Through his smile, Thorfinn would complain in jest,

"Erik – you cause my cheeks to ache in our endless laughter. How could such a dear ally force this pain upon me?"

"I give you no apology, Thorfinn, as your ugly face needs *any* sort of adjustment!" Erik usually mocked father.

"HA! Not to worry, for I will return the favor, when we meet again, my friend."

On occasion though, he was the brunt of insults and snickering by several of our neighbors who held a lessened loyalty to our name than their predecessors, at times with selfish or even spiteful intent. From the intolerant few who wore blinders to Thorfinn's rationale, he was viewed as foolish, and harsh words were spoken. Once, a pompous neighbor of ours, Armod Beard, rudely questioned my father – and in the obnoxious manner he conducted most of his conversation in.

"Why not just *buy* your family a thrall, Thorfinn?   Hilde's talents can surely yield enough to afford you a slave, you stupid fellow."

Father was selectively deaf not to notice such judgments. Especially from one as Armod, a man of whom he often warned us.

"Beware of shaking hands with Armod, for as he pats your back, it may be with his blade rather than his palm – he is one who speaks from both sides of his face. Beware of his intentions!"

Considering they were strangers on their wedding day, my parents tolerated each other quite well, and our home would easily fill with laughter. Sometimes after our *náttmál,* our evening meal, as all went quiet in the night, Hilde would tease father about how it took some time to accept his unusual habits once they were married.   Thorfinn, being the playful man he was, would immediately return Hilde's sarcasm with some quick wit of his own.

"Well, not to worry wife – when I selected my bed-slaves, they quite enjoyed my unusual habits." This was always laughable, since *everyone* told how father never purchased any bed-slaves. Mother would smile and brush off his comment, as she announced to anyone in company it mattered not if he *had* selected a concubine.

"Hmmm…jealousy is not a word I know, husband. Besides, if it meant I would then have some help with all the weaving and sewing, I would *gladly* offer up the twelve ore for you to have your bed-slave! Why not buy two?"

Their indifference did give way to a friendship of sorts over time. I once caught them behaving as if they had possibly even acquired an attraction to one another. I remember well, one night when they believed Helgi and I to be asleep I remained awake and quietly wandered away from my bed. I saw mother take father by his hand and lead him to the hearth-stone. She rubbed on a paste created from a healing herb called *hvonn*, asking him where he felt pain. Hearing him breathe out heavily, it was obvious father felt soothed and relaxed by the remedy, as well as Hilde's touch. She reminded him as she playfully nudged him, how he was her favorite subject in all that ailed him, and the two laughed amongst themselves.

While she was away performing her paid duties, father, brother and I remained at our farm. Mother was regularly sought out for healing assignments, whether by a neighboring farmer, wealthy landlords, or even noblemen – they were all commonly in need of her gifted counseling or consecration.

I enjoyed very much listening to Hilde recount the tales passed down from her own mother, and I wondered if things were for her as they were for Rena. Mother was a wonderful storyteller, and my favorite stories she told were of the travels of her mother's mother, Rena, and the grandeur she bore witness to.

"There once was a beautiful wife of a wealthy Earl, who was surrounded in silver and gold pieces. It was she who gave up her very seat next to her husband, for your grandmother. Rena feasted with their court, and was treated as royalty, and she was respected in her wisdom…" How Hilde's eyes would widen, and her face brighten, as she spoke. The excitement in her words made the tales all the more special and important.

37

The accounts recalled how respected and exalted the *seeing* women once were; but as time went on, they were becoming less appreciated.

Rena, and her mothers before, were women of distinction. I was told how the reputation of a prophetess also served as a defining characteristic, for although it was widely known the capabilities of a völva, many were viewed as being 'different.' Their profession was like a sword with a double-edge, since the very same quality making them unique also set them apart. If a woman practicing the art of seiðr did so carelessly, the outcome could be dangerous, or even deadly. Völva or not, one could become the unfortunate victim of ill will by a poisonous or even hostile master of seiðr.

My first experience with such malevolence was when I was but seven years in age. Mother had been visiting the home of her brother's widow, and was gone a day's time longer than expected. I was in the grazing field near to our home, seeking some sheep that had gone missing. All appeared natural and orderly, until the quality of the air in the grassland changed to a thick and heavy feel. I stopped where I stood, remaining still and aware as I sensed something was amiss. Strangely, I suddenly felt very drowsy and without any control of my body, I lied down in the grass. Immediately submerged into slumber, I fell rapidly into a dream-like state. Curiously, I also had an odd notion of being awake, and my mind was left with the impression of being stranded between the two realities.

Alerted to a dark figure moving slowly toward me, I looked over to the forest surrounding the pasture. The edge of the woods were distanced enough to cause my heavy eyes to stare in focus, while close enough to easily identify the dark gray face of a horse as it came into my sight. To my surprise, the animal remained steady on a slow yet deliberate pace, in the direction where I rested. As it entered more into view, I was frightened to see it moved as if under water, while the eyes were a glowing red. In each step, it reared up brutally then landed its hooves down violently. I attempted to call out for help in hopes my father might be able to hear me, but no sound left my open mouth and my heart thumped fiercely. Unable to rise up from the ground, I became frantic. My helpless body could do nothing but anticipate being trampled by the horrifying creature. Suddenly, a familiar voice called out, loudly and angrily, to the unnatural horse.

"HALT, Mara – you ugly beast!" It was Hilde, interrupting the moment. Her nostrils were flaring, and her tone authoritative. She thumped her staff to the ground. With each thud into the earth, the wand's rhythm matched her rhyme.

"Go now back to the lair,

"Filled with the foulest air,

"From the malicious seiðkona who sent you,

"Whom must be tamed, and renounce you,

"I will avenge this day, beware,

"Leave her at ONCE Mara, you wretched mare!" Hilde ended her words, by pointing her wand directly at the horse. I was in disbelief as I watched it mysteriously evaporate.   I ran to mother's protective arms, all the while amazed at what occurred.   With the fear still fresh, I trembled.   Promising she would always protect me until I no longer belonged to Thorfinn, mother whispered,

"Shhhhh, let me comfort you, daughter. Do not be afraid any longer, for I have sent it away.   Mara does not belong here, let alone coming at you, and I will seek revenge.   Child, shhhhhh….it will be all right…I will make it right."

The following day, mother held true to her promise and pursued vengeance against the völva who had been so dark to send the nightmarish beast. These things Hilde did remotely, while in a trance-like state, within a deep, hidden portion of the forest belonging to the goddess Frigg, near to our home. It was considered Frigg's sacred *skógr* by Hilde, and was shown to her by her mother. In this place, mother would enter and meditate upon any case presented.   Frigg's approval, answers, or recommendations helped mother find resolution, among other things.   After learning of Frigg's opinions, and if it was right to proceed with prospective quests or any other such campaigns,

Hilde was never one to argue. She knew and understood – it was her fate to follow the goddess' direction.

Leading up to my youth, the affiliations from generations before gave way to decades of brewing grudges; but even so, my life remained uneventful, and quite typical until one day in my fourteenth year. This was the day when everything changed.

A group of the King's men came to collect Hilde. The men informed father she was being retained by Norway's King Erik, known as 'Erik Blood-Axe,' to join a small band of traders he was sponsoring. The men insisted she must travel to Kaupang, the great trading town found to the west of Eida Skog, on the shores of the North Sea.

Thorfinn was advised Hilde could sanctify the sales of the men on their voyage, since the past two expeditions had been disappointingly fruitless. King Erik was not only losing his patience but also his wealth, and he was not one to take either loss passively. With their abundance of squirrel furs and other hides, the King's traders were unsure if they had possibly been cursed. Mother was to depart with the band from Uppsala, with the ship's bow pointed east then south, as they sailed along the waterway passage of the Volga Trade Route. Hilde was told she would eventually reach their destination in Constantinople, within the famed Byzantine Empire.

"…But I do not understand – why are you bringing my wife to Kaupang in the west, only to turn and travel east, for Uppsala? Must she sail from Kaupang, and then on?" The men had no answer, only ordering she must go or they would burn down our hall. Frustrated, father and mother had no other choice than to grant the King's wishes.

And so off she went. I watched as she disappeared out of sight, along the road through the forest. I remember her smiling back at me over her right shoulder. As I returned her expression I had not the slightest inclination – there was no way of knowing this was to be the last time my eyes would look upon her lovely face.

CHAPTER TWO

Someone Wicked

Time had passed, and it appeared as if Hilde was either lost or dead. We knew in our hearts abandonment was not the case, although the idea sat upon whispering lips of the few who turned their heads at Thorfinn, Helgi, and myself.

"Gossiping fools." Father would calmly mutter, without giving them any further attention. We held hope for Hilde's safe return, but just as storm clouds cover a bright sun, fear of something sinister slowly overshadowed our faith of her invulnerability.

Father remained optimistic by outward appearance, filled with stoic confidence; but in his heart he crumbled with grief. He missed her with his entire soul. As each day the sun rose, so did the feeble quiet, old man he became. The task of keeping our farm was a more daunting one, and father decided to pay for the assistance of five men and one woman.

Several days after we celebrated the yule-tides, on a wet, blistering morning, someone approached our home. It was Hendrik, the eldest son of Erik, our nearest neighbor and Thorfinn's closest friend. Upon his arrival, he requested to have a moment to speak with father. Our house-carle, Harald, told him of Hendrik's wish.

"Hendrik is here? Why does he not just enter and speak with me?" Thorfinn asked Harald. He was confused as to why Hendrik's visit was being performed in such a formal manner, when the young man's father was his own equal comrade.

"He did not say. He simply requested a moment to speak with you. It appears to me to be an official request," Harald coughed subtly, yet obviously so, while gesturing to me.

Now it was apparent to us all: Hendrik had come to ask Thorfinn if I may wed him. Surprisingly, father seemed to become agitated as he motioned for Harald to permit Hendrik inside.

"I bid you good day, Thorfinn," Hendrik announced as he bowed his head in salutation.

"Good day to you as well, Hendrik. Your father and mother are faring well, I hope?" Thorfinn asked, as he had not seen either of Hendrik's parents since we had last seen Hilde, almost five season's past.

"Yes," Hendrik smiled "they are both well, indeed... "

The moment between words spoken became stagnant, and Hendrik seemed to shrink into the planks of our floor. His feet shifted, and I could almost hear his breaths quivering.

"Sir, I have come here today to ask more of you than a simple greeting. I have come to ask…" Hendrik grew pale in color and was unable to even point his face in the direction where I stood, beside Thorfinn. Helgi now entered the house and approached Hendrik, throwing his arms around him as if to compliment his achievement.

"Have you decided when, or do you prefer to attend a Thing to get the official opinion?" By a *'thing,'* Helgi was referring to assemblies regularly held to discuss important matters, by and for our people. Kings were chosen and elected, laws drafted and confirmed. It was also at such a meeting advice or direction would be given or received. In this case, leading to the decision of an official alliance – as in two families to be united in marriage.

I knew Hendrik very well, as our fathers had been very dear to each other. And after all – when I was born it was Hendrik whom father planned to have me marry. He grew to be quite tall and strong. Hendrik had a face very nice to look at, but not what to make of it, and blushed, more often than not, when in the company of women. In spite of it though, I thought him to be a very kind but shy boy. He met such description, as he bashfully answered my brother.

"I have yet to ask your father, Helgi." Now turning to father, Hendrik pulled breath through his nostrils, to his chest. It made him appear as a man, to me, for the very first time since knowing him.

"Thorfinn Bondesson of Eida-wood, friend of my father, I have come today to ask of you your daughter, Helga. I request your permission to have her wife me." Father's response shocked every person in the room, and I watched as Hendrik's smile slowly vanished from his face, into a look of dismay.

"No, Hendrik – you may not," Thorfinn stated very passively, but with contention. He turned away from us and walked outside. He dismissed the notion and himself, without another word.

"Hendrik, you must understand. He has not been the same since our mother…" the words became too heavy for Helgi to speak, so I took the initiative to complete Helgi's perspective, trying to explain our father's puzzling disposition.

"Thorfinn has lost himself, since our mother has yet to return from her travels, Hendrik. It has been a difficult time for us all. Please leave us now, but the best we bid to you and your family." Our families would always depart in good will for one another, and each with happiness in their hearts. I wished for Hendrik to leave this day, with the same sense of warmth. I smiled to let Hendrik know that unpleasant wishes were not the intention, and walked out to pursue father, leaving my brother and Hendrik behind.

It was revealed Helgi encouraged Hendrik to go home, as soon as I was far enough away. He suggested for Hendrik to try again, after time was had to convince Thorfinn of my release. Helgi felt the unity of our families would be the wisest choice, and my becoming the responsibility of another would lessen the burden upon him and my father to survive. It was the way we all had to thrive, as our days were toughened with depleting supplies necessary for continuity.

I was held up as I searched for Thorfinn, sinking in the deeper snowdrifts. In my haste, I failed to secure my snow-shoes as I went after father, and they soon detached from my feet. This left me very uneasy in the terrain. After following his ski tracks in the snow I caught up with father, deep into the wood near to our land. He was approaching the dense trees of Frigg's Skogr, the sacred place my mother frequented.

My cries seemed to go unnoticed, as I called out, "Father....! Father, please stop and wait for me..!" My pleading had no effect, as father continued on without hesitation. He stealthily slid toward the largest of the snow-covered stone markers, placed in the earth ages before by those unknown. The stones served to distinguish the boundaries of this solemn space. I watched as he threw himself onto the wet ground near the great tree, so large in size that it kept its leaves through each season, and dominated the Skogr. I could hear father's cries as he wept.

"Frigg...Frigg, please," he spoke through his sobbing, his breath steaming in the frigid breeze, "...PLEASE tell me where she is! " He did not notice a tepid wind as it began to blow, swarming the falling flurries, but only around the trees surrounding us.

"As each new day I awaken, my heart struggles to beat. I must know where she..."

"Your wife has been slain, precious Thorfinn," an inhuman voice abruptly answered, loud and penetrating from our ears to our insides. My flesh sprouted each strand of hair, as I was overwhelmed in awe. For there she now stood, the goddess Frigg. With brilliant, red locks of hair falling over her pale green skin, she settled at two times high the stature of my father. I could see her pouch, also red in hue and filled with garnets and herbs – it rested around her waist. She wore a white garment, wrapped around her feminine form. Her feet were bare but clean, poised just over the icy ground. Yet as imposing as she appeared, her presence was not one of fright, but rather ... of radiance.

"Did you permit it, goddess? Are you not the one she would have called out to, as her life left her body?" Father probed of Frigg, seemingly unafraid, but with due respect.

"Her plight was not directed at me, but I was present as she left your plane of life, dear man. No – she called out to *Mist*." The goddess answered, and again with that unusual voice, that sounded like many voices in one. It was distinctly unlike any intonation my ears had ever heard before. I could feel my body trembling, as I hid behind the tree I settled near when Frigg first appeared. I assumed I was concealed from her sight.

"Mist? I do not understand…why? What occurred on the day of her death? How?" Thorfinn asked, still with tears falling from his eyes.

"Someone wicked decided our beloved Hilde to be a liability, and chose to extinguish her breaths. He tightened his hands around her throat, laughing as she fought to respire." I heard father cry out in anguish, as I felt a twisting in my gut, and I wept quietly.

"Although I know all ørlǫg, I am also known to not speak of it. Even so, have no doubts. The woman, 'Mist,' she sought, is she!" In an instant, and faster than I could process, Frigg's arm rose with fore-finger extended, indicating where I stood. Her eyes pierced through my being, with a white glaze covering her pupils, giving them a silverfish stain. Thorfinn glanced over to me, perplexed, and in shock. Startled by my exposure, I turned and began to run. My feet carried me away swiftly, but a song contained in a breeze followed and stayed with me, until I raced passed a stone marker. Now, all that could be heard was the snow packing beneath my sprinting feet, and my shallow breaths.

I kept my pace, running all the way back to our farm. When I arrived, I did not want to go inside the main door. Rather, I entered through the rear entrance and decided to go sit with my young horse, Boulder, in the stable portion of our house. The smell of the hay and the oats was comforting to me, as I considered Boulder to be my most devoted friend. He loved me invariably, always appreciated my company, and never squabbled...nothing more could I ask of one whom I loved, animal or not.

I did not want to see either my brother or father, although I knew Helgi had seen me run through the rear door. He and Leifr, another of our house-carles, were making repairs to our largest sledge. Leifr planned on departing soon, as he drove a sleigh pulled by our strongest oxen to fetch wood for fire.   This had been Helgi's duty before Thorfinn paid for help, and I was glad Helgi no longer had to perform the task. I now feared for his safety deep in the woods. I no longer trusted another after this day. Hearing Frigg's description of the wicked one who took the life of mother, I felt violated.

After my head lie rested on Boulder's mane for what felt like an entire day and night; his neck jolted, and he stamped his hooves, in a restless way.   Something, or someone, had spooked him.

"Helga?" I heard Hendrik's voice call my name, and wondered what sort of trance I must have been in to not have heard his steps enter.

"Helga – I wish to speak with you, if only for a moment. So please… do not be afraid."

"What would I be afraid of?" I appeared behind him, and he whisked around, quickly. The weight of emotion after gaining knowledge of my mother's fate held me down, and it felt strenuous to even speak. However, it was obvious that I had startled Hendrik and could not help but to smile at the look of his abashed face.

"It appears as if you are the one who is now frightened, friend." I said.

"Whew… ha!" Hendrik tried to laugh it off, but we both knew he was genuinely startled. "Helga, you take my breath away – in more ways than one!"

"Um...Hendrik, you mustn't try to beguile me, after all these years of knowing our fathers' wishes." I felt flushed and unsure from the charisma Hendrik now attempted to woo me with. I was not accustomed to such advances.

"Are you not willing to accept my proposal, even though Thorfinn now protests?" Hendrik had a look of disappointment in his eyes, and I genuinely pitied him; but I knew I did not want him as my husband – arrangement or not. With father no longer holding this wish in his heart, my viewpoint would be accepted.

"Hendrik, please know this – I think you are a *wonderful* boy, and..." I stopped, as I noticed the term 'boy,' made him look away from me in humility. I rested my hand upon his arm in comfort, and corrected myself.

"Pardon me. A wonderful *man*. But with this said, to make such a decision…well, it…it would not be a fain choice, and I would need it to be. Hendrik, I must be willing and eager to marry, whether it be you or …or *Boulder*, here!"

I had hoped my illustration would demonstrate that it mattered not *whom* I was intended to marry, but rather if I felt it to be the best decision. However, my explanation was not received correctly by Hendrik's surprisingly limited understanding.

"You…you would marry your horse, Helga?" He asked, meekly. Staring into his face, I raised my brow in astonishment. I was baffled, not only by his question, but also his apparent lack of comprehension. After all, it was not as if I spoke in riddles, and I considered the concept to be a very transparent one. I was moved simply to blink my eyes, seeking focus, waiting for this unusual moment to pass. I greatly appreciated this back and forth now, as I was even *more* satisfied father did not permit me to wed such a child-like man.

Through my smile, I offered relief,

"Hendrik no, I would not marry my colt. The meaning of my example is that it matters not *whom*… If I am unready, than I choose not to force such an issue." There was a moment of awkward silence, as slow-witted Hendrik still sought to interpret my choice of words.

Realizing it was likely best to just say it out-right, I clarified my answer for him.

"I mean to tell you 'no,' Hendrik. I will not wife you, my kind friend." I looked at him, while expressing myself gently, as I sincerely cared for him, but not in the way he wanted me to. How things would have been different for him if my father had agreed to the overture.

"Yes…fine. That is fine." He beamed at me, and I matched his expression. "Not to worry, Helga. It is you I wish to husband, and give me time. I will show you it is a choice well to make. I will return." Hendrik's eyes remained fixed upon my face, as he walked out of the back exit. I stood there, still, with a bewildered mind. The dazed character must have still been apparent on my face, for when Helgi neared the stall I stood in front of moments later, he noticed my confused state.

"Sister..?" he asked, "Why do you look as if Boulder asked to you to marry?" He gave a brief term for me to react, then laughed at his own parody. I shook my head in further disbelief.

"What an unusual day, yes? First Thorfinn's reaction, then Hendrik returning, *followed* by his strange puzzlement. Thinking you are deciding between him and your horse to marry!" Helgi laughed on.

"Ah, then you heard our conversation, I gather?" I was comforted to know I was not alone with the idea of how strange this all seemed.

"Yes, I did. I admit it was difficult not to overhear. And where is father, since I remember you chasing after him, into the snow? Leifr will be going to collect wood soon, and father possesses our single best hein stone – I want to sharpen the axe blades."

"He did not return, after I?" I was unaware Helgi had not heard of what Frigg explained about our treasured mother, earlier.

"No, he did not. Not to worry, I can just use another whet stone. Helgi stopped to look at my face, then asked, "Why do you gaze at me in this way, sister? Your eyes are filled with grief."

"Helgi, Frigg showed herself to father, in her sacred wood. I witnessed it, for the first time, and could hear their talk…" It was very challenging to reveal Hilde's demise to my brother. "…and father asked Frigg what the fate was of our mother, and if she still walked the earth." I stopped to draw in the courage to continue on. I knew Helgi would be met with a devastated heart. But also, knowing him as well as I did, I was equally certain he would not voice his sadness, yet keep it tucked away while it consumed him.

As I had predicted, after I had confessed all that I witnessed, Helgi's posture uncoiled and the muscles in his jaw clenched tightly. He spoke through his grinding teethe.

"And *who* was this wicked one Frigg spoke of?" he asked.

"The goddess did not disclose, brother."
It was painful to watch Helgi's temperament
change, but his anger and distress was expected.

"Remember this day, sister. I will make
it my mission to hunt this man down and receive
justice for our mother. How *dare* this beast of a
man, to take the life of such a loving woman as
mother!" He exited the stalls with the energy of
a storm, throwing down the axes he held,
grunting from the force he exerted.

And as peculiar as it was, I imagined
Hilde in my inward eye we all possess when we
close our lids and let ourselves really *'see'* how
we feel. I envisioned her looking down at us and
nodding, as if to agree with Helgi's proposed act
of vengeance – similar to the day the Mara beast

came at me. It must be made right. We would

seek revenge and make it right.

CHAPTER THREE

Magic of the Runes

We kept all of our animals, even our swine, penned within our home during the winter so they did not freeze. On the morning following the day of Hendrik's proposal, I was feeding food scraps from our dagmál to the pigs kept for slaughter. The time made for our *dágmál*, or the day's first meal, came after commencing our duties around the farm and our home upon waking to the day, when a healthy appetite was found.

"Helga!" A loud whisper called out to me from the back doorway, from outside. Surprised, I spun around so quickly I almost fell onto the young piglets in the pen. It was Hendrik, and he was holding his hand out for me.

"Hendrik…! Why do you ambush me in such a way?!" It felt as though my heart jumped into my neck, he alarmed me so.

"Oh, delicate girl – my apologies for startling you in such a manner!" He seemed sincere, so my attitude softened enough not to heave hen shells at his face. "My heart holds deep sympathy for you and yours. I have heard of your mother's end from Helgi, and I wish to help." I looked down at the floor wishing to avoid the very talk of my sadness.

Hendrik further explained, "I have brought you something special – something I have made for you to help you manage your ailing grief."

Excitement was in his eyes as he passed me a small, yet solid piece. I examined it and realizing from its jagged edges yet porous quality, that it must be bone. From its size I deducted it to be whalebone, which I had seen before. Upon it was carved symbols I knew to be runic in nature. These runes were designs patterned by my people to relay a tale, document an event, or even summon a charm upon its owner. I did not know how to interpret such inscriptions and was puzzled, yet delighted by the engravings.

"What do they stand for, Hendrik?" I questioned, without seeking sight of his lips while he answered. I was suddenly enraptured by the runes.

"They...uh, they are..."I hadn't noticed Hendrik stumbling over his own words, as dishonest people periodically do, "they are to bid you well, and keep you well, my beautiful Helga." Hendrik answered me, still in a whisper. I smiled as I studied the bone, but was too amazed by the gracious souvenir. "I will go now and leave you to it." I was still captivated so, I barely understood he was going on his way back to his home.

"Hendrik! …Hendrik?" I called out, upon noticing his disappearance.

"Yes, Helga?" He was back at my threshold, in a moment's notice.

"I thank you for thinking of me." I finally was able to pull myself away from the small, beautiful gift, and expressed my gratitude while peering into his blue eyes. He looked pleased by my thrill with him, and in the object he awarded me. Then, he hurried away.

Unsure of where to keep the endowment, I placed it upon my cot, in the apartment where I lay down each night. After returning to our hall, Thorfinn stood where Hendrik had just been.

"What did Hendrik need, Helga? By the time I had seen it was he departing on his sleigh, he was too far off to call out for."

"He graved runes for me in whale-bone, father. He said they were to help me with my ailment," I ceased speaking, as I felt the twisting cramp in my gut again.

"You are ill, Helga?" He asked curiously, and I was unable to look into his face. "What is it that ails you, daughter?" He questioned gently. Thorfinn was a competent father possessing many life skills, even fostering the emotional needs of his children.

"Father my heart aches. Mother..." I attempted to verbalize my deep sorrow.

"Yes, I understand. It will all take time daughter. It is known that another woman I should likely wed....rather I now pay Nadin," referring to our efficient house-maid, "to satisfy your mother's role. And too, you do quite finely weaving and contributing on the farm." Thorfinn paused, then reached out for me. "Come to me, daughter." I went to him, and into his embrace, and felt safe again.

The day progressed into night. I began to notice an unusual level of discomfort entwined in fatigue, and I looked forward to rest. Before retiring for sleep, we sat in our hall going over what Frigg had told. Father and Helgi tried making sense of the ordeal, and we speculated who it might have been that murdered her.

"Master Thorfinn!" Leifr suddenly burst through the entryway with heavy breaths, but was overcome with relief upon seeing us all.

"Leifr, what is it that you fear? Was all not right with you, as you collected wood?" Father and Helgi rushed to inspect Leifr, unsure if he may be injured. Upon standing I became dizzy, and rested back into my seat on the bench.

"No, sir…" Hunched over, Leifr still breathed deeply, and made effort to explain. "I passed men… numbered in six… all thickly outfitted… with weapons…" His words were fragmented between his laborious panting. As Helgi helped Leifr over to the fire to warm himself, I chose to find sleep in my apartment. I found balance by holding onto the walls – all the while, recognizing my condition to be quite strange indeed. My body dropped unto my bed, causing the whale-bone from Hendrik to slip to the edge and fall onto the floor. When reaching for it, I only pushed it further under my cot. I decided to leave it lie, confident I would regain my health in the morrow. Then, I would gather up the whale-bone.

During the night, my dreams were of a disturbing kind, and my body tossed and turned seeking comfort. When I had finally succumbed to slumber, I was only to awaken as my sweat soaked through my bed-clothes. I awoke midway through the twilight, and thought I noticed another in the room with me . . . but was startled to find I was completely alone.

"Was someone in this room, just before? *Anyone?*" I screamed out, questioning the night. Finally father found me. He rubbed his eyes while he studied my demeanor, befuddled.

"Helga...?" he carefully questioned as he cautiously approached, "what troubles you, daughter?" Thorfinn's body looked twisted, and his shape blurred into shadows. I closed my eyes, wishing not to see my dear father in the way he appeared to me now.

"Sorcery?" It was all so puzzling, and I feared all sensibility had left my reasoning. Maybe Thorfinn knew of what had suddenly haunted me.

"Helga, please rest your head. So much has transpired until now, that time must be had to absorb each event. Rest." And Thorfinn walked into the darkness. I was unable to nap, and watched as the walls warped and melted. I awaited the sunlight in hopes it would put an end to the reality I now saw, and to this insanity. Whistling and ringing fell upon my ears, and slumber was not achieved.

The next morning, it was nearly impossible for my legs to hold themselves steady. Helgi carried me to the daïs at the end of the hall. There I sat, perched on the bench like a sickly old maid, as I unwillingly held onto maddening thoughts.

Without warning even to myself, I hollered up toward the ceiling, "We live in a land that has gone *completely* irate, with one too many acts of senseless hate!"

"Helga!"   My father scolded me. "Daughter, you quiet your tongue! There is *no need* to yell in such a manner."

"Uhhh...! Father?" I cried out while holding my stomach, which churned in pain. "Please forgive me. Please... help me!" I begged of him and felt all control lost, as I urinated where I sat. I began to shudder, and I wished for my mother's presence – longing to have her hold me and ease my worsening situation.

"Oh, my child...!" All at once, my father was filled with concern, and rushed to my side. Our house-carles Ringmar and Benki joined him, as they called out for Nadin. The men propped me up, and Nadin loosened and took away my soiled garments. I was carried to where she could easily cleanse and re-dress me. Then I was lifted back to the daïs, where I could stay under my father and Nadin's watchful eyes.

I feared a disease of my mind was slowly encompassing it; and without hunger to feed or thirst to quench, I knew I would become lifeless soon. Unable to contain any part of myself, I uttered more nonsense.

"These ideas...and all of this conformity..." I announced, "they distort into a *tangled* reality...like every great generation that has come before now, to the gods of destruction *we must* accordingly bow!" Pouring from my mouth and knowing not where they, or their sponsoring thoughts, originated from, I *knew* I was delivering most unusual rhymes. Everyone looked at each other, mystified. I however, found it to be most terrifying.

Another day came to pass, and Nadin now stayed with me as I lay in bed. I hoped to be alleviated, as I beseeched Frigg in prayer, begging for sleep. But just as the night before, my body remained irritated and in distress. Finding no relief, I remained awake through another night, and without calm.

Dawn approached and Otmar, our trustworthy work-dog, began to bark uncontrollably. We knew this meant a stranger was on his way and within a moment it proved to be true. The shuffling of many feet was soon heard, and grew louder as they ascended up the hillside, nearer to our home. I detected the sound of metal clanging in each stride, along with heaviness in their steps and it was obvious: whomever now approached was adorned in swords and such. Then, over Otmar's low growl, I heard father's voice outside. His voice was faint but still audible.

"Is there something that can be done for you? I see that you hold weapons, and we are a peaceful house." Thorfinn spoke.

"We are searching for another is all, farmer. Tracking their sleds in the fresh snow, we seem to have lost them." One of the men answered.

"Not to worry – we will go away, down your hill from where we came, and leave your home untouched." Another promised.

"I thank you. Good travels to be had by you all." Thorfinn bid them farewell as they left our land.

"Father, do you know who those men were?" Helgi asked now, as he stood guard near Thorfinn.

"No son, I do not – but since it is evident that blood they do seek, I am glad they have moved on from here, and without incident."

As the two entered our home, I overheard Thorfinn mention me to Helgi.

"Helga's body and mind needs peace. She appears spell-bound, but in a crooked way…" Helgi remained quiet as Thorfinn thought aloud. "I should hope Hendrik's runes bring her relief, and quickly. " My attention soon wandered away from their talk. I then watched as the morning sun cast light on the wall.

A little while later, I was once again seated in the end of the hall on the daïs. Oddly, I quietly sat there, just observing every one, and everything. It was as though I was strictly of spirit, and alone. I felt as though I was detached from all that I had previously *known*, and all I once perceived to be real. Helgi came to sit beside me, but said nothing once he was next to me. His eyes grew wide as he watched me. My senses were overpowered in disgust, as I smelled something foul. It appeared I was the only one noticing the pungent odor, when I inquired, "Do you not smell this putrid scent also, Helgi?"

"A putrid scent?"   Helgi repeated, questioning me. Inhaling to search for any such stink, he answered me. "No, Helga – all I smell is the meat and the curd we are soon to have. Sit with us, sister.   Perhaps you will find your hunger, and appease it?" Helgi reached out his arms to assist me. "Come, I will help you." But I declined. I was too weak to move from the bench.

Just then, Otmar began to bark once again, and vehemently so. We knew another was moving up the hillside, toward our home. The uproar our dog exercised had everyone stop immediately. I was certain Helgi even held his breath, if only for a moment, as he looked over to my father and then to the house-carles. Up they all stood, and gripping each his axe. Helgi walked over to our entry way, while Leifr, Ringmar, and Benki followed. Harald drew nearer to Thorfinn, and Nadin came to my side. Suddenly, we were all surprised as we heard a man's voice from outside call out.

"We seek the land-owner named Thorfinn!" He yelled, but in an unimposing tone. No longer did they feel threatened, for in an instant, father went out to greet the strangers with Helgi and the house-carles.

"That is I, sir. May I be of assistance to you?"

"Yes. My name is Egil Skallagrimsson, and these are my men. Weary from travel, we come craving a day-meal and to bait our horses." The man spoke respectfully.

"I would gladly grant this, Egil. You may all enter my hall to rest and sit at meat." Father granted the man his request, leading the way inside. Benki and Harald tended to their horses.

I barely noticed the strangers as they entered and warmed themselves by the fire. The leader of the men, the one called Egil, appeared to have a scowl on his face. I thought he might be angry, as I did not see too much detail of his features. However, I gave it not another thought, as my aching body doubled over.

A moment or so after the men thawed, they sat to eat the meat and curds. The men were starved, and they spoke not a word at first – only taking short breaths between bites.

"You were called a 'Worthy Man,' and now it is evident to me, *why* that is." His hunger fulfilled, Egil conveyed to my father happily.

"I am gracious for such a compliment." Thorfinn pleasantly responded. "Whom is it then, I must thank for such a kind description?"

"The King's men," Egil explained, "who have joined my party. Have you seen anything of them?"

Thorfinn shook his head, to answer that he had not. This was all very suspicious, as the King's men whom regularly travelled the roads we lived near to, were now dead. They collected tribute, or money, from the farms of Eida-wood to give to King Erik Blood-Axe. Recently, and on their last mission, all twelve men were robbed and slain. To now hear that new men were directing someone to our farm was very questionable. No sense could made of this matter, and I suspected the supposed new 'King's Men,' were indeed only people made to confuse, or even harm, Egil and his company. I could tell my father thought the same, but he did not let on. It was his way to gather information, *before* making assumption or passing judgment; so he spoke not of his knowledge, to Egil. Egil continued to explain how he had come about our farm.

"We split our party, below the ridge and just past where the roads divide, on the day before last. They went on to the nearest house of Arnold, to lodge, and we – elsewhere. And then, we appointed to meet here."

Shaking his head a second time, my father realized the men who had come upon our home earlier were not whom Egil sought, either.

"Here passed six men, together, a little before day: and they were all well armed." My father advised.

"I was driving a sledge in the night to fetch wood, and I came upon six men on the road." Leifr added. "They were house-carles of Armod Beard, a wealthy land-owner who neighbors this land." Egil nodded, as if to imply he was already aware of Armod. "He lives up yonder the ridge, just as you go over it, in a large house. But that was long before day, when I seen these men. Now, I am not sure whether these will be the same as the six of whom you spoke."

"Yes," Thorfinn said, "and the six men whom I had met, passed *after* my house-carle, returned with the load of wood." My father pointed to Leifr, in order to show Egil, which house-carle he was referring to.

A brief period elapsed, as Thorfinn acquainted Egil with Helgi and the rest of the household. I let out a faint whimper as I squirmed in discomfort, attempting to find a better position that I might rest in. I fought hard the urges to shout a harsh shrill, or allow my limbs to strike out impetuously; but soon lost, as I felt as though every bit of my spirit was being devoured by delusional thoughts.

With my eyes closed, I began to whisper.

"In an ocean of uncertainty, we hesitantly wade, and we wait.

"While our souls are lost in a blur of fury, we want any shimmer of glory…to the end of our ordinary story…"   Opening my eyes to gain sight of where my father sat, I noticed him and Egil, both peering over at me as they spoke quietly.   I strained to hear their conversation. Just as I was able to hear the commotion and dialogue earlier, outside, I listened to their words, even as muted as they may have believed them to be.

"That is my daughter, Helga. She has long been in this sad state, and complains of a pining sickness. She mourns the loss of my wife, her mother, named Hilde. This past night, no sleep was gotten, and she has been…as one possessed." Thorfinn described my behavior, as Egil studied me curiously.

"Has anything," asked Egil, "been tried for her ailment?"

"Runes have been graven," said Thorfinn, in a despondent tone, "a landowner's son hard by did this, and she is since much worse than before. But can you, Egil, do anything for such ailments?"

"Maybe no harm will be done by my taking it in hand." Egil replied, looking at

Thorfinn, then at me. He took his last bite of his meal, then a long sip of mead, finishing it off. Pushing his seat out from the table, he stood up and walked toward me. With each step of his boots, I heard a booming sound. His steps echoed thunderously and resonated in my ears, in torment. Clutching my head, I covered my ears to protect them against the deafening noise his feet made. It stopped, suddenly.

"Helga?" I jumped, unaware that he was very near to my face.

"My name is Egil. " He quietly spoke. I now saw there was no scowl upon this man's face, but a deformity of his skull-bones. His crown was elongated, and it pushed his flesh down, nearly covering his left eye. A handsome man he was not, but the earnestness in his stare overpowered his expression.

"Yes – I have heard, as you and Thorfinn, my father, conversed. What…" my chest began to rise and fall, as I struggled to contain my sentiment, "is it that you can do for me?" I lamented in shame, and to be in such a state of debility, I began to wail. I yearned for my sickness to cease, and the hope I saw in this stranger's eyes brought me to tears. I hushed my own mouth, for I knew to fret not. I would not perish, and truth sat deep in the gaze of this man Egil. He smiled at me reassuringly, then turned his face to Nadin, beside me.

"I bade you to lift her from her place, and lay clean clothes under her." And they did so.

Next, Egil asked me where the whale-bone with the engraved runes was. I told him it was the only piece I had, and the last I remembered seeing of it was under my bed. He went to search under where I had lain, and found the artifact, just as where I had said it to be.

With a careful grasp, Egil closely analyzed and turned it to view every speck of the inscriptions. His face drawn in burden, Egil looked up at us. Taking his blade from his side, he struck the whale-bone and began scraping off the patterns. He did this over the fire, allowing the shavings to be burned up. Egil then cast the entire bone into the fire-pit once they were completely erased.

"House-maid, take each of Helga's bed-clothes and hang them out to air." Adhering to his direction, Nadin followed his command with urgency. We all easily gave our trust to his apparent knowledge of the runes.

Then Egil closed his eyes, and began to sing,

"Runes should not be engraved, *ever*, by anyone who knows not their interpretation.

"For without intending, their meaning might be a chant of darkness,

"As in these ten rune-words, spelled wrongly in this inscription.

"In the whale-bone these carvings remain,

"Gifted here, to this herb-serving maiden,

"Now causing her such deep suffering and pain…"

He then graved new runes, into flat piece of wood gotten from a tree near our house. Egil laid it under the bolster of my cot.

All at once, the diabolic fever that had ravaged me lifted!   I felt as though I was awakened – and out of more than sleep. Helgi and father were overjoyed. I was at last comfortable enough to eat and drink, then I retired for a short nap.

Thorfinn graciously offered all the fealty and advocacy to Egil he might *ever* be in need of. Egil accepted this new allegiance, then told Helgi and father the full happenings on the night before coming to our home.

Egil and his men indeed had known of our pretentious neighbor Armod Beard, for this was where they had lodged.

The guests, Egil and the other three men, were tired and hungry. For two nights straight they traveled along steep passes, even becoming lost in a blizzard, until arriving at Armod's.

None of us were surprised to hear of Armod's inhospitable conduct. He fed the famished Egil small amounts of stale food, only to save the better provisions for himself. Armod's youngest daughter whom we all knew to be a kind and right child, sang a song to Egil at her own mother's beckoning. The verses she sang revealed her father's ill manners and bad intentions.

We were disquieted to hear Armod then slapped her so strongly she fell to the floor into the blood dripping from her little nose. Hoping to divert from his devious act, Armod insisted his servants bring out his best meat for Egil and his comrades. Egil was offended to a high degree, and acknowledged he sought to redeem his respect before going on his way the following morning.

Just before they were to depart, Egil boldly walked right into Armod's apartment and pulled him out of bed by his beard. With his sword drawn, he sliced Armod's beard from his face. He shaved very close to his skin, then crushed one of his eyes. Egil admitted – in his anger, he wanted nothing more than to slay Armod, but with his wife and daughter in company Egil opted not to. Then he and his men fled, arriving upon our home this day.

"We should be on our way – let us continue on and leave this family to recover from their ordeal." Egil spoke to his comrades, deciding it would be best to carry on.

"Egil, you are a great man of many talents, and you are quite complex. You have options of fighting battles with words *or* iron. Your ferocity is volatile," I was now in the hall and spoke directly to Egil. I had awoken from a dream, having had a vision of this man. I was compelled to confront him with my knowledge.

He stopped and turned to look at me as his color changed from typical to the fairest white. Egil was puzzled, as was I. Slowly, his hand gripped his sword, and I could feel his temper begin to boil.

"Helga – hold your tongue, daughter! You mustn't disrespect the man who-" father began to reprimand me when Egil interrupted.

"No friend," Egil appeared more curious than angry, and as he let go of his sword he said to father,

"Please, allow her to continue...I am intrigued." He raised his chin at me, motioning I carry on with my talk.

"...My point is here made, for you can find the pleasure or the insult in any given moment." I began to step closer to where he stood, unafraid of the images I *saw* in my mind. He was aggressive and unpredictable. I could *see* him as a child, maybe in his seventh or eighth year, plunging the blade of an axe into another boy and leaving him dead. But I remained unafraid. His heart was forceful, and he was destined for greatness. I knew harm to me or mine he would not commit.

"The lineage from which you spawn is a glorious one, Egil: grandson of Kveldúlfr, the 'Evening Wolf' and very wise, shape-shifting Viking. It was he that owned much land from his plundering. You fled to the Land of Ice with your father, then returned...and here you now are. You are talented in words, a gift that gains you options in battle, for you may utilize them or your sword. Either way, you will surpass and succeed. You will be spoken of for centuries beyond today." Egil was speechless but honored.

"But be warned: The King's messenger's friends," I continued, as I allowed my mind to purge its knowledge, "…they were told to slay you. And the party you are seeking to join up with after you leave here? They have deserted you. The ill-meaning men await you now in the wood, and with weapons ready. They are expecting you, be assured." I finished and inhaled, as I was winded.

"How did you know all of this, Helga?" Egil questioned me. Breaking my eyes away from his, I subtly shook my head – I had no answer for him. I did not know how I knew, I simply just knew.

"Did you tell her of this?" Egil asked, looking to his companions. They were equally confused. I had obviously revealed knowledge that none of us were privy to.

Egil looked genuinely unnerved. Here this great man of many lands stood in front of us all. He who was known to viking, and frightened of no one was now at a loss for language and decision.

"*How* do you know of this I ask?" Egil came close to me again, and I was suddenly intimidated by his obvious disturbance. Looking now quietly threatened, his demeanor changed. Fear had not been something this man could define, or even perceive.   After an awkward silence, Egil then drew back and smiled once again.   This time his expression was of amusement and resolve.

"Ah...I see."   Preserving his smile, he looked over to Thorfinn then back to me as he conceded, "You are skilled in *seiðr,* are you not?" The room was hushed.

"Yes," Thorfinn surprisingly spoke up.

"She must be. I have heard this sort of talk before from her mother, Hilde." Father looked over at me, staring for a moment.

"...And this has all been occurring as Hilde once prophesied it would, long ago. In a song she sang to me after returning from Frigg's Skogr one particular day, she divulged: Helga would not grow to marry Hendrik, Frigg would mention her but named as the Valkyries ride, and she would soon *see...*" My father stood over me, unaware of how troubled and anxious he appeared.

In this brief, yet stellar-in-impact period in our time and in our lives, significant indeed it all was.

"The magic of the Runes can be disputed by none, my friend. A gate has been opened by them this day. Such is the fate we Norse live by, and in it all, purpose was had. Our paths needed to cross this day, and I promise to make mention of this whole occasion one day, Helga Thorfinsdotter."

Turning away from me, he slapped Thorfinn's back. Helgi joined in the intimacy of the bit, by patting the chest of our father after a handshake with Egil.

As I watched the men speak about deciding the next course of action for Egil, their talk faded from my ears. I was drawn to go and sit near the fire, suddenly captured by the hypnotic flames. Slowly I began to see the shape of my mother's eyes. My entire being swelled with happiness, as my spirit suddenly grew with ambition.

Looking into the blazing colors, I somehow *knew* what I must now do: travel to Gamla Uppsala and make sacrifice at the Dísablót. This was the year for the Disting festival to be had, one was held very ninth year. Coincidence of all these things was none.

However I was unaware of what things must occur first – I had a new endeavor in the making. I was to embark on my new path in life as *völva*.

CHAPTER FOUR

The Messenger

Time had passed, days not numbered in many, with an intensity of things to come. Much like watching the sun in the warm seasons as it travels across the sky, from left to right, as it completes a days' time, I felt as though I now lingered, awaiting something significant yet not knowing how, or even why it would come about. That is, not until the day *she* came.

I had been weaving with Nadin just before mid-day. Such work became mundane, as my body knew the method so well I needn't even be mindful of the series in actions required. But true to my character, I somehow always found my mind sinking into an abyss of deep-rooted thought, and falling away from the actual task at hand.

I watched Nadin as she seemed like a slave to the large wooden framework of our loom. It leaned against the wall lazily, while she tiredly walked from one end to the other, obediently, and with each pass of the thread. Nadin remained silent as I observed her. She always became so engrossed in her work, and on this occasion failed to notice Otmar walking into her path. She caught herself from toppling over him, landing into the wall the loom rested upon.

"Haestpeis!" Nadin cursed at him under her breath, unaware I heard her remark.

I nearly choked in surprise, immediately appalled but mostly amused, by the name she chose to call my unconcerned pup.

"Nadin...!" Astounded, I was at a loss for words and struggled to withhold my laughter.

"At least you could label him the *correct* animal!" I confronted her selection of titles for Otmar as I stroked his rough hair.

"Otmar, don't mind Nadin – she meant to call you a dog's penis, not a *horse's*...! I promise to remind her of which you are." I assured him while he kept on his course and away from me.

Reading an equal amount of amusement in Nadin's smile, I watched as she tucked her silver hair inside the knotted kerchief which sat upon her head. Her hair reminded her youthful complexion of its true age. As I looked on at her, my thoughts wandered off yet again. I imagined all the seasons this woman must have known in her lifetime until that very moment. Condensing her lengthy existence, my mind pondered a parallel between her and the long process of fabric-making itself.

Such an effort began with the rearing of sheep, permitting enough time for their coats to grow long enough to harvest. Just as it took seasons for Nadin's mind to develop and body to strengthen, while striving to sustain itself.

Then came the shearing and cleansing of the wool. We boiled the wool to refine it, removing all the earth and bits, similar to Nadin coming of age and washing away any stains in her character.

Next came combing and smoothing of the tangled wool with a durable, iron-toothed comb - Nadin would have matured quickly, sifting through the necessities needed to endure her arduous life as a servant for the wealthy.

Followed by rigorously pushing through, and pulling out narrow fibers down the spindle, as it churns round and round. Thus was the cycle of her survival: coming within reach of rest and freedom, only to fall back into labor and servitude.

So was the end result - thread to be born, as well as all that encompassed the experience of Nadin - the integrated woman, learning for herself every skill and talent mandatory to keep her life ready for another dawn.

Finally, fabric was weaved upon the very loom Nadin now paced in front of. ...Much like the portions of her continued life: cutting and sewing bits into a garment to be worn, and Nadin was left with a patchwork of knowledge and understanding.

My thoughts ceased, and I arrived back in the moment as Nadin's expression changed from calm to fright. I could nearly smell the fear she was now drowning in as she stood there frozen.

"What... Nadin?" I asked her, unaware of what had abruptly alarmed her. She did not speak although I noticed her attempting to. With her hand shaking, she pointed to the threshold of our hall's main entry. I turned my head and was almost immediately filled with the same shock Nadin now displayed.

A woman now stood in the doorway. The wind howled behind her, yet no draft or chill aired through the open door. Her face was slightly hidden by the hood of her black *slædur*, or cloak. It was most unsettling that Otmar hadn't warned of a newcomer approaching, and I wondered where he might have possibly gone to. Then to my absolute surprise, I saw Otmar standing near this woman's feet. His tail fell between his back legs, and his head was low to the floor. I had never seen him in *any* sort of submissive state, which only compounded my confusion and fear.

"May I enter your hall?" The mysterious woman asked in a quiet and smooth tone. The residual weight of her voice could still be felt in the air. The corner of her mouth became visible and I noticed a soft grin laying upon it.

"Yes…yes, of course. Please do come in from the cold." I reached out my arms in the direction of the glowing flames, motioning that she should warm herself. The woman did not seek the heat of the fire, and instead walked closer to where I stood.

"What are you doing - who are you?" I questioned her, feeling more surprised than afraid as she approached me. Stepping back from her, I finally felt myself reach the wall behind me. This stranger now cornered me in own home, yet I was not insulted or enraged, as I likely should have been. I heard Nadin gasp, catching my attention, and she had a helpless look upon her face. Holding a blade to threaten the woman, her arm was controlled and suspended above her. Something unseen was now preventing Nadin from harming our new guest, who remained a hand's distance from me.

"Do not make any menacing moves toward me Nadin, as I am not here to endanger young Helga. Lay down your blade, house-Maid," the unusual woman ordered firmly, while keeping her back to Nadin, who now stood glaring at her. Nadin's arm was then released by the invisible energy, and she complied by resting the knife on a bench near to her. Nadin looked outraged and horrified at the same time.

I closed my mouth when I realized it hung open in astonishment with the unfamiliar woman, and the things she just voiced. How unique indeed was every last detail of this woman. Her dark cloak was a hue I had never seen a robe dyed before. The method to color clothing in such a way would be nearly impossible from what I had ever known. Even stranger to me was its length, causing the garment to drape and drag behind her - yet it remained noticeably dry and unsoiled. It was not practical, for one would continually stumble over the fabric. It would certainly be more of an obstacle, tangling and pulling underfoot - but it didn't - it stayed perfectly in her shadow.

Her face became more unveiled, and I could see markings covering her lovely features. One of her eyes showed from behind her hood, and I observed its bark-like tint. Remarkable curls of a color that looked similar to a leafless branch. Stained upon her skin were pictures of tree limbs. Without being aware of *how* I knew, I was certain they were symbolic for Yggdrasil, the ash tree at the center of our Norse universe.

Yggdrasil served as shelter for the nine worlds of existence known to my people, linking all perfectly. The same world tree's gallows from which Odin hanged from during his trial by initiation. He did this for nine days and nine nights, in his quest for knowledge.

"Who are you, and how is it you know our names?" I asked her as I looked at Nadin, who stared shamefully toward the ground.

"I just *know*." She smiled again as she continued. I held onto every word she expressed, in complete awe.

"My name is *Gna,* and I was sent to deliver you, Helga. Freyja sent me. She told me you were *ready*." She drew in a deep breath, and I waited to hear her exhale but heard nothing. I could feel my heart beat with uneasiness as I asked my next question.

"She sent you to collect me...*what* exactly, am I ready for?" I felt I must be told what this was all about, although within me I *knew*. Hearing her answer, I was validated.

"It has come time for you to sacrifice your lower self to your higher self. Be it known, I give you three days to prepare your belongings, for you may or may not return." Gna turned from me and walked to the door from which she had entered only moments before.

"You will need to be prepared for your journey, Helga. On the third day, and at High day - I will return for you." And just like that, Gna was gone. Her cloak vanished into the breeze, for when I looked out after her nothing could be seen.

"Helga..." Nadin now spoke up, but quietly, with fear still underlying in her tone.

"Do you trust this woman calling herself 'Gna'? Or do you think it was your fylgjur guardian spirit, bringing forth an omen of some sort?"

I knew Nadin well enough to know she felt slighted for the way Gna thwarted her attempt of attack. In all of her seasons, Nadin still had yet to master the art of hospitality. Yet she was trying to protect me, and her selfless act touched me.

"Nadin, thank you for your willingness to guard me against any intruder. You are most loyal and dependable. However, I do believe her. I can accept Freyja sent her."

"Hmm...!" Nadin remained unimpressed. "Well, I hope Master Thorfinn returns with Helgi and the house-carles sooner than later. I am not as trusting as you are; and with all of the recent activity, hostility can be expected. *Someone* should stay behind to defend you in any case, as my frail old body would surely crumble under the force of another," Nadin explained as she held her arm. She walked passed me to pick up the thread she dropped when she first saw Gna.

"He'll return soon enough – less than the full eighths of daylight, I should think. Nadin, I have much to do if I am to be prepared for the third day. Come and help me gather all I will need..." And as she always did, she walked hastily to gather my cloak without wasting another moment. We quickly got about to the task of preparing.

Father, Helgi, Harald, and Benki had last been seen when they went out to escort our guest Egil and his men into the woods. I was confident no harm would befall them, and they would arrive home shortly. Besides, Armod's men knew well enough the brutal vengeance that would most definitely befall any of them if they had.

Upon Boulder I planned to ride, and I prepared the load he was to carry accordingly. My saddle was made from leather, with a frame of wood. Sacks could be carried from the high pommel at the front of the seat, and the cantle to the rear. I had four sacks in all, each equipped with its own mounting ring, to hang from the pommel and the cantle. Thankfully, many items could be kept in each. I suspected that it might be best having two of each garment. Clothing was a prized commodity, and the season was still in winter.

I began with a spare linen under-dress and over-dress, always held on with shoulder-straps. Connected to each of the straps were four brooches in total, one for each side of my shoulders. Covering the front of the over-dress, I wore several strings of my favorite and precious glass beads between them. They were gifts brought back for me by mother.

I hanged many useful tools from these beaded strings, such as my whet-stone, tweezers and ear scoops. From my braided belt hung two different knives, and my tongs. Designed by Hilde were special pouches made with loops, and held on by my belt. In these satchels I packed my quartz stone for fire-making. In a smaller leather pouch, I kept a bundle of seeds, all hemp and the same I knew mother often used. Included was a small, tight roll of extra thread, and needles for garment repairs.

My *höttr*, the hood covering my head and down my shoulders, would be essential to survive the wintery weather. Nadin did well to thread extra linings of fur into my cloak. I thought it best to bring an extra home-spun covering made from sheep skin. Leg wraps helped to keep the lower parts of my legs and feet dry, but Nadin suggested I include longer socks for my feet and gloves for my hands. She worked so fast, before I knew, Nadin finished the task of weaving these for me. She did this quickly by needle-binding. Using this simple and swift technique of knot-weaving, Nadin produced a garment nearly impossible to tear; since each knot was stitched so closely to the other. Nadin reminded me how fortunate I was.

"It is good for you, Helga, Master Thorfinn can supply you with proper socks," her eyes looked up at me, as her face remained fixed in place. "As long as I can remember, since being a child - even as recent as taking up work at this farm - when the need arose, I had to stuff my shoes with grass or hay. I had no socks." Most families, such as the one Nadin was born into, were poor, without easily affording thread for such luxuries as socks.

Benki was skilled in tanning hides into leather and Nadin easily found several thick pieces to thread to my boots, ensuring better coverage of my socks and leg wraps.

Moving on to the final necessity, I went into the food storage space next to our dining hall. I would bring enough food to last me no more than three days - all dried fish. Fish was plentiful and we kept it stored in vessels, while more hanged from the rafters to dry. To best preserve the dried meat it was salted.

"Daughter, why is it you need these fish? And where exactly are you going, as I see you are packing things?" Thorfinn's voice cut through the rope of thoughts I had become entangled in.

He looked at me inquisitively, shadowed with concern.

"Father, someone came for me while you were gone. She said Freyja sent her to collect me, and will return the day following tomorrow. I was preparing…" I explained then looked around at all of my belongings stacked upon one another and scattered about the floor.

"What a mess I have made, I can see. I became so set on my plans, I hadn't noticed…." I allowed a moment for father to speak, but he continued to stare at me with a surprised expression.

"It will all be packed away rightly, I promise… so not to worry."   I ended my explanation sounding more like a question, as his silence was slightly unnerving. I don't recall even a single blink of his eyes, as he peered down at me. His arm rose, and his hand drew near to my face.

"I need you to sew up my sleeves, daughter." The cuffs of his shirt near his wrist were stitched to keep drafts from finding their way in. I became puzzled – did he not just hear of what I had informed him? This was the strange behavior my father increasingly displayed since Hilde left that fateful day. It saddened me to watch as a stranger consumed the man I once knew as my father.

"Father, did you –" I began to ask as if I should repeat myself, when he spoke over my words.

"Yes daughter, I heard you – Gna will be collecting you two days from today, and she will be the one to deliver you to Freyja…I know of it all." He did not even look into my face as he spoke. Rather, he watched on as I quickly finished stitching his second wrist. He spoke loosely, almost with an undertone of boredom.

"Mm - thank you, it feels much better." Father finally looked into my face with a smile, then turned and walked away.

"Are you not at least *surprised* in my going? I must say - this is not *at all* how I thought you would react to my news." I resisted my laughter, motivated by my anxiety. After all, I did not want to appear as if I had gone mad…*again.*   Thorfinn approached my items and knelt down. Then, to my relief, he continued to pack them up. He calmly spoke.

"Daughter, I was waiting for this announcement. I am aware of ...the *way* in which it must occur. I mean to say - the way it is done. You were finally...ready."

I had to remember to breathe, as it was uncomfortable the way father mimicked the sounds of Gna's words to me exactly, and in such a way I would have thought he had actually been present for her visit.

"You see daughter, our lives begin as seedlings. As we grow, we must be fertilized to grow even further. This day was foreseen by your mother and she described it *just as* it is happening. I know Gna will take you to sacrifice yourself…" my father deeply exhaled, then continued on, "to *yourself.*"

CHAPTER FIVE

Remain Fierce

It was the third day as I waited for the sun to sit at its highest, and the moments moved slower than a settling glacier. Boulder had been packed efficiently with my many supplies. Our home was shaking with all the moving about - everyone with something of importance to show me or provide me with. I was overwhelmed with the invasion of ideas and orders. When Helgi spoke to me about Boulder's hooves and walking in the snow, I understood why he thought I was not minding him.

"Helga, be sure to sharpen Boulder's spikes on his hooves often enough. Use the axe blade - like this - and push down to the ground. Be sure to only sharpen in one direction: down. Helga...?" I heard him, but was consumed with so many thoughts I did not voice a response.

"Sister – did you hear what I have said about Boulder's spikes? It is important you remember to whet them with your axe."

"Yes brother." I finally spoke out. "I have heard: whet spikes often with axe, point blade away from myself, sharpen only with blade down...yes?" I decided to take a moment to look at his face, then continue on.

"Yes - you are correct." Helgi answered, stood up and walked out of the hall. Father did not waste another moment accepting a turn to give direction.

"Daughter - lend me your eyes as I show you how best to keep your axe hidden in your cloak." I watched Thorfinn cross his right arm over to his left hip, next to his left hand holding his axe. This was all to be under his imaginary cloak, of course.

In an instant he pulled his right arm up, wielding his axe and struck down while he said, "*Down* onto his left shoulder, and still down as you move across to his right side...!" He stealthily positioned the axe head face up, while thrusting the blade across, from left to right. He even acted out his opponent's role as he went on to explain.

"…and as his right arm now holds his left shoulder, in painful shock… that is when you slice directly into his exposed right side…!"

"Be sure to strike *hard*, Helga - and fast. As hard and fast as you can. This way, you do not even allow enough time for your enemy to unstrap his sword!"   Such a simple yet effective maneuver. I was amazed by my father's speed and battle wisdom.

"Do this in need of protection, *and* in defense. In an ideal moment, just go straight for his head! But always remember to strike hard. If there is time, we will practice more movements outside so you are well acquainted with the tactics. Helgi and I will demonstrate the stunts for you, so not to worry. I will leave you to it since Nadin has something for you. When you are finished with her, come out, daughter."

Nadin was standing by, waiting patiently to show me two small pots, both with clamped rings to hang or handle them by.

"Helga, use these to soak your leeks and hvonn and such – they are for boiling. They are very useful to have and easy to carry. Ringmar has included four leather canteens, two small and two big." Nadin held out her arm to Ringmar who stood behind her. He put in her hand the straps connected to each of the four vessels. Nadin explained,

"Remember to fill them each opportunity you have –"

Ringmar suddenly interrupted Nadin, "- and be sure the water you fill them with is always freely moving, girl. Never use water lying stagnant."

"I see. How do I set them? By making an oven out of stones and resting the pots upon it, or…?" I had never had to boil water away from the hearth in our home.

"A good question you have asked." Nadin answered. "Benki gave these leather twines for you. It might be easier to find small logs or solid branches, and tie them together with the twine. You can easily assemble a frame to hang the pots by, from the rings used to hold them. Like this - do you see? You just place a log through here…connect more as legs to each side…and it will sit similar to this." I watched on as she showed the way in which each branch would sit to suspend a pot over a fire.

"The twine is strong enough to hold shelter fabric as well – line it between trunks and secure the edges." Benki added before Nadin resumed.

"Oh – I also have these pockets to collect herbs and such. And here - this drinking horn, as well. The inside was coated with bees wax this past summer - it does well keeping the taste of the bone from your drink."

"I am gracious for your guidance, Nadin"
Calling out to the doorway, I shouted, "Benki and
Ringmar – you as well."

"Helga, Harald has several long pieces of
hemp rope for you. He has Boulder outside and
will show you." Ringmar had entered after I
thanked him, and informed me.

Donning my cloak and fastening it, I then
walked out into the crisp air. Father and Helgi
were holding weapons and called me over to
them.

"Helga! Take up that shield and axe!"
Helgi yelled out to me as he pointed to the
weapon and shield.

"Watch father and I. I will act as...."
Although my eyes looked upon them, my mind's

inner vision took over and all I could see was Gna. All else, the activity and the voices, seemed to fade into the background. I was quite satisfied, feeling as if nothing had been overlooked. I felt I was, finally, prepared.

Suddenly, we all heard the trumpeting of an unfamiliar horse off in the distance. It was, no doubt, that of a stallion. But to my absolute surprise, the horse rode out from the sky.

"Just as in the way the Valkyries fly..." I thought aloud. My brother asked I repeat myself, when a hushed voice was spoken.

"*...they fly through the Mist,*" I heard whisper on the wind, while we all watched as Gna and her horse come closer.

"I *heard* that! Did you hear it as well Helga?" Helgi questioned and looked at me with his eyes as wide as his lids would allow. "It answered you – the wind! It said *'they fly through the mist,'* did you hear it as well?"

"It fell upon my ears also, son." Father spoke for both he and I. I looked around at each face as they gazed up to the sky in awe. The expression of shock masked each of us, and we all looked on in disbelief.

We saw the trumpeting stallion as it galloped from the heavens. With his nose held high, he shook his neck and proudly fluttered his tail. Throwing his hooves about, he lowered himself and Gna down to the edge of the field. As he still tossed his legs and hooves about wildly, the youthful horse glowed with energy. He and Gna settled a small distance from where I watched. Looking at father to somehow bid him farewell, he rushed at me. I was startled more as he grabbed my arms and squeezed them tightly.

"Daughter – I must tell you: *remain fierce*! You must remember to *never* show fear, and hold your ground. Never run, or you will die tired!" He paused a moment to make sure my eyes were watching his.

"I underst-"Without realizing he was not finished with his thoughts, he spoke over me.

"Helga- never forget who you are and from *whom* you come. You are my daughter and there is *much* to be proud of!"

Turning away from every one, I mounted Boulder and went on my way toward Gna and her horse. They waited for us in the field. I was nervous as we grew closer to where she waited, and my eyes met hers. Although I knew she was not human, I trusted her as if she was kin. She bowed her head and smiled, then rode off. My entire body grew numb and I felt detached, much like I was dreaming. It was as if I traveled not within my own body, simply watching from above.

"Do not allow anyone in – to your mind or yourself, daughter!" Thorfinn warned.

"Always   hold   your ground...REMAIN...FIERCE!"   Father screamed in such a way I had never heard him before. I imagined it was the sound a warrior makes when he hollers out in battle. Thorfinn - my father, my protector, my provider... I listened as his words carried on the breeze and disappeared into the open air. I prayed to the gods it not be the final time I would ever hear his voice.

CHAPTER SIX

<u>As it is above, so it is below</u>

It was quite extraordinary, the many emotions I was experiencing as I left behind everything and anything I had ever known. How strange indeed the previous few weeks had been. Even still, as I thought about it all, it was surreal. Never in a hundred years could I fathom I would be embarking on such a fantastical voyage - being collected by Gna, and in order to be delivered to Freyja.

Boulder followed behind Gna's horse, and I was amused to notice her horse throwing his hooves about wildly as he cantered. He looked like a young child, dancing excitedly without a care.

"His name is *Hófvarpnir*, Helga." I heard Gna's voice, but not in my ears – rather, in my mind. Startled, I knew not what to make of another's sound in my head. Naturally, I had believed my thoughts alone could be the only to dominate my perception. If I only knew, from that day forward the many whispers, cries, and tones from others I would begin to *hear* in my own mind.

I followed Gna and Hófvarpnir as they led me on a familiar path through the forest.

Passing each tree, brush, and stone, it became clear to me our destination - Frigg's sacred wood. I wondered why we had settled there.

"Frigg will bring you to Freyja, Helga. I am simply her messenger..." Gna's thoughts entered my mind again, answering my question. She halted Hófvarpnir and dismounted, leaving him to rest himself near to us. I did as she, and Boulder also moved to where Hófvarpnir stood. With her right arm Gna pushed back her cloak, as her left hand outlined a circle. The motion was fluid, much like all of her movements. I remained stunned as a round blue flame appeared, its spark brought about by Gna's gesture. The flame contained itself, and sat just over the frozen ground. I watched it in all its hypnotic appeal. As the allure of the fire pulled me closer, it was nearly impossible to keep my eyes from looking away. Paralyzed by its rapture, the world around me began to dull and disappear.

"Helga!" Frigg's unmistakable voice infiltrated the euphoric moment. My body jumped, and I turned to see her looking down at me. Never had I been in the company of a god, and I was overtaken by her almighty authority.

"Y-yes goddess…" I found it difficult to speak in her presence.

"Helga - do you fear me?" Her voice boomed and echoed off the empty tree branches. She looked at me with a commanding gaze.

"Yes and no, goddess. I do find myself uneasy in your company, as you are wife to Odin, reside in Asgard, and are the principal among the Æsir. However, a part of me feels contentment, for you are my kin…" Frigg looked down at me, her emotionless stare as icy as the earth beneath us.

"Hilde taught you well enough, Helga – your flesh and the blood that surges through your vessel – yes, it all began with me. It is also the reason you must be sacrificed, girl." She stepped aside as her right arm motioned to a labyrinth made of stone, behind her. I was perplexed, for this had not been found in this area before, and I had not seen it when I initially arrived with Gna.

My eyes grew wide seeing the elaborate stones marking a pathway through the maze to its center. At the middle of the labyrinth a vacant blue cloak hanged. It looked as if it waited to be occupied. The garment was identical to the one my mother always wore.

"As you enter the mouth of the labyrinth, keep to the right, and set your pace towards your goal at the center. Walk the labyrinth, Helga." Frigg whispered in my mind, and I turned to see her but she and Gna were no longer there. Searching for Boulder, I found him to be standing alone, and where I last caught sight of him resting next to Hófvarpnir. Drawing my breaths in for courage, I approached the labyrinth. As I entered, I did as told and walked to the right. My feet moved slowly and cautiously. I paused to study my surroundings upon hearing a near inaudible drum beating. My senses were on alert.

As the sounds manifested yet remained quiet, my ears began to notice a man humming with women chanting, and all matching the odd rhythm of the drum. I shivered in bumps around my entire body - how supernatural and eerie it all was.

Walking through, then around each direction in the labyrinth to its center, the voices and drum beats became louder and more magical. I drew nearer to the blue cloak, which still remained unfilled and suspended. I decided I must have been dreaming- how else could all be so twisted? All sense of reality was lost, and I was submerged into another realm altogether.

Finally, I reached the middle, and idled in front of the mysterious cloak. Not knowing what to expect next, I felt an embrace by unseen arms. Releasing the breath I held in, it was a relief to have the comforting touch. But suddenly, the mood changed from a moment of reprieve to one of trepidation.

"Augh!" I choked, as my head was forced up with violent strength, and my neck squeezed. The invisible energy gashed at my eyes, and *oh* the pain! I screamed out in complete torment. In that fraction of a moment, rushing thoughts sped through my mind.

What was happening? By whom was I being attacked? Do I give in or fight?

As I struggled to set myself free, a sudden sense of calm saturated the blanketing terror and I was able to drain the anxiety from my mind.

The sting of my blood streamed from my wounded eyes, and I let go of any control I had left. I surrendered, deciding my only option was to accept my fate. I would now die.

Without warning, the force released me and I fell to the ground. Its remaining energy encompassed my body, standing me up. My feet finally lifted from the ground, and it was difficult for me to even comprehend the many sensations I was feeling – both physically and mentally. My physical agony and the fear ceased, as my mind grew more determined and alive. The powerful force of my consciousness now guided me.

Strange while purely natural: I became acutely aware of passing into another state of actuality. In this balance of cognitive existence, one must utilize their mind alone. Understanding this, my spirit moved with great speed through a tunnel of sorts, rushing faster and faster until…it just stopped.

All went still, all went quiet. Standing on the edges of these two realities, I was amazed by the ease which I could travel in spirit alone, completely shedding all physical awareness. To my elation, I had just accomplished a skill known by all seiðkonas - the passing between two realms of being - and I was fascinated with my new feat.

Compelled to open my eyes, I cast them down - only to see I now hanged from the great tree in Frigg's skógr. Dispirited, my fear returned as I watched the tree suddenly come alive. Its branches slowly began to move and bend like arms. The wood popped as it cracked and twisted about itself, then around my own body. I let out a shriek as sharp and broken branches twisted and punctured my flesh, while completely enveloping me. I was absolutely terrorized into submission as my body was pierced and entwined. I was being consumed by the great tree.

"Iviðia...I am in the wood," my voice whispered, but I felt not as I spoke. Remaining within my body, it dawned on me - this was the point where I may or may not return...at all. This was the sacrifice.

Bewildered, I hanged there, unable to make sense of which direction I was held in. There was no longer up or down – I could no longer differentiate between the two perspectives. The branches high above could just as well have been the roots far below. I had no way of knowing.

"As it is above, so it is below, Helga. It is I, Freyja. I have arrived to subject you to a trial by initiation, and witness your sacrifice." Her voice was similar to Frigg's, but with a likeness of its own – I had the honor of hearing the voices of the gods.

"Your perception needs balance if you are to complete and survive this initiation." I heard her voice echoing in the opaque bark I found myself a part of.

"I ask you, Helga: what eats as it grows, but dies when it drinks?" My eyes could not see her.

Noticing the all-familiar glow and crackling sound, I was alarmed to see I had been covered in flames.

"You must extinguish the blaze, or you will find yourself amongst the dead, Helga." Freyja spoke. Before I could make sense of it, I knew the answer to her riddle.

"Fire," I answered her. Immediately coming into view I could not resist the three wells of water appearing suddenly before me. I sought to douse the flames I was bound by, and approached the water holes. Reaching out to the far left, I noticed water being poured into the pool. As I tried cupping the water with my hands, it was to no avail as it fell through my fingers and dripped back into the well.

From the middle reservoir I again attempted to bring water to myself. Startled, I quickly pulled away my hand in fright when a large animal fang became visible. It had pieces of tree root covering it, as if it was chewing the base of the tree. Just as quickly as it became visible, the monstrous tooth disappeared and sunk out of sight.

I quickly moved on to the third spring, to the right. Coming slowly into view was a man. He held a musical horn which he used to collect some water. Holding the horn out to me, he whispered.

"My name is *Mimir* and I am the *rememberer* - the wise one. Drink from my horn, for I am rich in knowledge and wisdom. Drink…" I accepted the horn and drank from it. The flames that had engulfed me vanished, and when I looked up to see Mimir again, he was no longer there.

Closing my eyes and re-opening them, I found myself hanging from the great tree again. I simply lingered there for an eternity… or perhaps it had been only a moment? I now believed the two concepts to be one in the same.

Suddenly, a sensation of being unbound came over me, and I was released from the tree's grip. Lowered to the ground, I was alerted to Freyja's voice as she abruptly appeared. The goddess towered over me with her light-colored hair draping around her shoulders, falling down the sides of her arms and her back. She wore a golden collared necklace, containing a luminescent jewel. It sparkled so bright, my eyes could not decipher its color or kind. Her expression was empty, and it was as if she peered through me.

"You have completed your initiation through the trial of fire." Her eyebrows raised as she lifted her head. "You have conquered death." the goddess spoke at me, through my mind. Her lips did not move, and her crystal-blue eyes stared down at me. Freyja's message continued,

"You have entered into the highest state of consciousness.   As you are in this supreme state, powerful one, you can now properly perceive the layers of your existence. You have awoken your higher self, and are now infused with its power. The balance of your being is achieved. Your essence has been reborn. You are no longer *Helga,* for she has ceased to exist. The name chosen for you is *Mist.* The Valkyries ride through and over this fundamental element, linking air and water. 'Mist' is how you will be known to *see* and give your prophesy, and for the remainder of your days in the west - in the land of humanity. When you expire, your grave will be fixed to the sunrise, east - the rightful plot for a völva as you.

"I release you now, back to your plane of existence – go now, Mist. Go now and *see!*" Freyja's final word reverberated through me, propelling me down to the ground. I closed my eyes as the spinning world around me set back into its proper place.

Awakened to Boulder whinnying, I lifted my head and wondered how long I had been lying there. My body felt numbed, finding myself lying on the ground in the goal of the labyrinth. Raising my arm to wipe the blood from my eyes, I was surprised to find they were unharmed, and I was able to open them. As I looked at my hand I saw the blue of the cloak - I was now adorned with the mysterious robe. The confusion in my mind settled, and there were no questions of who or why remaining – it was all accomplished as it was meant to have been.

Rising to my feet, I wiped the bits of dirt and gravel from my dress and walked out of the center of the labyrinth, to the left. I observed my environment as I once again walked the maze. I noticed the dark sky and the many glistening stars sprinkled among it. The moon was large and glowing, providing its light generously.

Making each turn and travelling closer back to the mouth of the labyrinth, I noticed a long piece rested at the exit. As I made my way closer, I was astonished to see it was a staff, with the length of a walking stick. Leaving the stone maze behind, I reached out for the iron wand. It was warm to the touch, and with a surge of energy it contained, I felt static fill my body. At the top of the staff, iron bars rose out into an enclosure, much like a small cage. The wand's squared length was also made of iron. I rubbed my fingers over the intricate designs and patterns etched into it.

My body quivered as I realized what I had just achieved.

"I am Mist…" I quietly spoke aloud as I held out my wand. My nostrils flared and my breaths hastened, as I was unable to control my excitement. Throwing my arms up to the sky in triumph, I shouted out to the world.

"I AM MIST!" Caught up in my bliss, I clumsily stepped back and misplaced my foot - part on the ground and part onto a small unstable rock. As the pebble rolled under my insecure foot, it caused me to drop clumsily onto my back, and down to the solid ground.

"Ooaf!" My victory cry ended in a whoop, as all of my breath was knocked out of my chest. Once I regained my breath, I could not help but laugh at my clumsiness, and facetiously muttered,

"*Mist* was chosen - not *Agile*..!"

I rose to my feet and approached where Boulder patiently waited.

"Hello, my friend. What a loyal animal you are, as you sit here." I rubbed his mane and cheeks while greeting him. I was happy to not be alone in the wilderness.

"I ask your opinion: would you like to carry on then?" I questioned Boulder as I mounted his saddle. As if he answered me, I continued our talk.

"Yes – two and a half's day journey.

Well, we will be there before long…I hope."

CHAPTER SEVEN

Uppsala

The rocking motion in Boulder's stride caused me to tire even more. I wiped my hands over my eyes to awaken myself. As my right hand stroked down my left cheek and onto my left shoulder, I felt the smooth fabric of the blue cloak.

My thoughts drifted to mother, and all of her accomplishments as a seeing woman.

Curiously, Hilde had never told of how she had come to obtain her signature cloak, nor was it ever revealed to me the story of her own initiation. I wondered: was it the same ritual had for each person, or was it always as unique as the individual?

Why hadn't I ever asked mother how she became a völva? I pondered. She had just always been. This only added to the mystery of the vǫlur - the *seeing* people.

Perhaps I would encounter another prophetess when in Uppsala. I was certain I would happen upon others such as myself, for the feasting and ceremonies were attended by a multitude of people, and some from the far reaching lands.

Father had been present for the feasts one year, at Gamla Uppsala. Thorfinn told Helgi and I tales of what his eyes saw. He told of the *dísablót* celebration in which a banquet and sacrifice was made to honor the *dísir*. The dísir were females worshiped by my people and known to be half goddess, half woman. They were known to some as the souls of the deceased, and to others as guardians of the dead.

The festivities took place for nine days, with each day involving its own agenda. An offering to the dísir was one man, then dog, sheep, horse, oxen, goat, moose, hen, fox, or the like whilst ending in feasting. Also was the large market filled with goods, jewels and food.

Finally, the Thing of all Swedes took place. Raids and the plan of action for the upcoming warmer seasons would be outlined: who would be going off to viking and where, which ship might they board. There was much to be decided upon.

My attention was brought back to the moment just as I heard a wolf howl, off in the distance. I hoped I could move swiftly on and without incident or delay.

Examining the sun's position again, I determined it to be well beyond mid-day, and believed it to be the opportune time to make a camp for the night. It may take longer than expected, and I would rather have time to spare than not enough at all.

Reluctantly, I decided it was time I find a suitable site to build shelter for the reminder of the day. As I scanned the forest, I dismounted Boulder upon noticing a great fallen spruce lying a short distance from the path. I stepped around the large tree inspecting it and determined it was efficient in protecting not only myself, but Boulder as well.

Its trunk was as thick as Boulder's girth and I was able to touch where the tree snapped, standing upon the tips of my toes. The break was fresh enough so most of the branches remained thick with green brush, cascading toward the ground to make a perfect covering.

I brought Boulder over to the tree and removed my axe from my pack I had within reach, connected at his saddle. Heaving the axe over my head, I hollowed out a channel through the center of fallen limbs. I swung cautiously, using more power in the well-planned movements. I counted a number of branches, some large and small, some dried from exposure.

I moved on to the next task of priority: fire. After digging all the snow and moist soil out and leaving the heap out to dry, I chopped up the remaining branches. Positioning my touchwood cloth over the dry ground, I began to lay out the groundwork of feeding my spark. I searched my packs, almost in a state of panic, until I realized I had left behind a crucial tool to spark a fire: my strike stone. I stopped my rummaging and drew in a deep breath, as my mind remembered my walking past it on the daïs, saying aloud, "There it is - I mustn't forget to bring that strike-stone!"

Bringing myself back to the present moment, I spoke to the forest,

"Of course…I will think of something." I smiled a crooked smile facetiously, as I regularly sought to find the humor in a challenging situation, an attribute learned by Thorfinn. I found it to be quite useful to have a healthy sense of humor when pondering heavy weighing matters.

Boulder suddenly whinnied and I jumped, startled not only by his noise but by the convenient time he chose to address me, as if to heckle me and my nonsense.

"Hmmm…what to use, then…" I answered Boulder as I searched through the sacks. Holding my quartz stone, I grabbed my axe which I knew to be forged of iron, and hoped to contrive another adequate method to bring forth a flame. Situating the touchwood under a small bundle of dried brush, I began to strike my quartz against the corner of the axe blade, and awaited to see some form of spark. Hitting the two together nearly ten times, the friction made way enough to conduct the heat. A few shaves of spark-like material fell onto to the touchwood cloth, travelling to the dehydrated spruce needles and smoke suddenly appeared.

"Ha…yes! …done!" I yelled in conquest. Adding twig upon stick upon branch and bellowing the growing flames with my slow breaths, I systematically erected a near flawless blaze. Staring at my undertaking, I was as one enchanted. Such comfort can be felt in the delight when one succeeds at building their encampment. Single-handedly I would survive a night in the vast forest.

"Do you see?" Boulder came closer and walked over, while remaining a safe distance from the heat of the campfire. I smiled, as if with a sense in pride in my beast's initiative and instinctual know-how. Even my simple horse could appreciate the necessity in the element.

Noticing how the smoke rose from the fire, I was even more pleased to see it ascending into a thin column, indicating fair weather. It was satisfying to know a storm was not upon us.

"Now for my cot..." I once again declared aloud, as if someone were keeping catalog of my ventures.

Gathering spruce needles and framing a pile of foliated branches, I was well insulated and nestled into the deepest and most protected part of the shelter. Laying out the massive hide from a white bear Helgi offered me before continuing on, I wrapped myself in it and felt satisfied with my lodging for the night.

As Boulder chewed on the sparse edible turf available under the snow, I easily finished off two whole dried fish. Their remains I wrapped up and stored so as to not invite any unwanted guests - by way of a wolf or the like. It was refreshing to drink mead, provided by Leifr in his small light blue flask. Only a little amount of sips were needed to feel relaxed, while remaining alerted to any impending dangerous circumstances around us - only a few drops.

I felt established enough to occasionally doze off, but without permitting too length of a time to fall into a slumber. To keep the fire from fading I constantly fed it kindling, sustaining its continuance until the dawn of the second day.

Before I knew it, a new day arrived. Boulder and I had remained unharmed throughout the night. As soon as I would have it, I packed up in order to advance on our quest to Uppsala.

I was collecting the last of my items from the shelter to pack within a sack fixed to

Boulder's saddle, when I dropped my quartz stone. Bending over to retrieve it, it caught my eye when Boulder jerked in an unsettling form – something had spooked him. Realizing I had become so distracted with collecting and stowing, I had wavered my sense of safety in my environment.

Immediately standing, I turned around while moving as close and swiftly as possible to Boulder. My back now touching his, I reached behind me and felt for his reigns. Just then I heard a dog's low gnarl. I had been come upon by a wolf.

His growl halted and his ears moved forward. I hoped he had come upon us unexpectedly, and looked to see if he was accompanied by more. If he had been, it would most undoubtedly lead to imminent trouble, and was relieved to see none, other than him. I refrained from making eye contact, as I knew this to be the standard challenge to a wild dog, and I wished to do nothing of the sort.

Slowly I made my way around to Boulder's left side and pulled the stored fish remains out of a sack, then I climbed up onto Boulder's back and into the saddle. I threw the fish remnants next to the wolf, who surprisingly did not pursue any assault, and went over to scavenge the fish debris. I nudged and kicked at Boulder to go as fast as possible away, back onto the road to Uppsala. Where there appeared one wolf, another nine or ten were found. I would not survive if a pack besieged me - this I was certain of, and I swore not to stop until I entered the limits of Gamla Uppsala.

My horse was loyal and carried me swiftly on my course. It moved through my mind throughout the day of it being *lördag,* our weekly washing day, and I missed the conveniences of being at home even more. Since it was not in my character to obsess over things – either I do it or I do not - I chose to act upon my wish; and pulling free a small bit of fabric, I held it over the opening of the canteen to allow for it to slightly saturate. I continued to wipe down my face and neck with the damp cloth. Dribbling but a few more drops onto my hands, I ran them through my hair to complete the 'washed' perception – however little it might be. I finished my grooming by combing my hair and neatly gathering it behind my shoulders, under the hood of my cloak.

It came to my attention that I *must* stop, although I wished I had not had to. I must relieve myself and knew better to do in the lightest of day. Bringing Boulder to a halt, I dismounted and found a spot where the ground covering was sparse, if covered at all. Walking back to where Boulder obediently waited, I walked oddly, stretching my arms up and down to my legs. In that moment I understood how foolish I must look - perhaps being alone and unseen had its advantages. I went upon Boulder's back, prodding him on.

Surprisingly, the sky gave forth snow, and I looked up to watch it fall onto my face. The wind stayed calm, and the flakes fell softly and slowly on me. How surreal this entire journey had been until now, beginning with watching my father and Frigg in the skógr…till this moment. Until this time, my days were filled mostly with weaving and preparing food, cooking, additional weaving, and tending to the animals - indoors or out, followed by more weaving, before ending the day. Now how different things were, and only two days later. I concluded my life would *never* be the same. …And it proved to be so.

We travelled on, until reaching the road leading directly to Uppsala – it was made distinct by its posts, numbered by over a hundred and a half, and of considerably sized wooden pillars. They were set a little less than a faðmr apart. I was happy to see them, for I knew I was about to enter the boundaries of Uppsala.

The hour fell late, yet there remained activity all around. I dismounted my horse and sought out a place I might rest for the leavings of the stated day. As I meandered through, I came upon an audience surrounding a known *Porgrimr*. He served my people as a wondrous story-teller. I desired to stay and join the crowd watching, but I needed to find a spot to rest my body.

We wandered on still, now coming upon a group of couples drinking. This was typical to what we practiced in Norway as well. The idea behind it was if each man was singly paired with a woman, less flirting with another would occur, leading to no drunken jealousy among men. It was customary to prevent any altercations of sorts, at organized feasts such as this.

I continued on with Boulder, and passed men taking part in penalizing one of their own for *við sleitur* - known as drinking with restraint. Amongst comrades, men were expected to comply with the total opposite - willfully intoxicate themselves. From my up-bringing, the punishment one could anticipate appeared to be the same among the men seated there: the accused must appear before all and empty an extra cup, draining the horn dry. His excuses were amusing as he complained of feeling ill. His plights were pitiful at best.   Feeling almost ashamed *for* the young man, I continued away from the group quickly.

I finally admitted to myself I had no idea where to seek shelter, and thought I might as well produce my own. Fortune would have it in the form of an ideal location - I found refuge near the slaves.

"Ah…I am so grateful …" I felt too tired to complete my words. I slowly but successfully strung a line between the tandem trees and draped my 'great cloth' over it. It was the length of three faðmr on each side, and served well as a tent. I secured the sides with stones and gathered my padding. I succumbed to my fatigue as soon as I rested my head. Sore and tired, my body was actually comforted by the pebbled terrain, and I was soundly sleeping before I expected.

I awoke the following morning well passed the typical time for dagmál, leaving myself with a sense of laziness. How different indeed it was, not contributing to my household. The security within that had always ignorantly been taken for granted until these past few days – this was all very evident to me, as if knocking me in my face.

Eventually, I purchased a boar from a woman at the market and was able to offer my sacrificial gift. The dísablót was indescribable to witness. I watched on as each being given up to the dísir was done away with quickly.

It began with a man who stood up and revealed his markings, front and back, indicating which clan or region he represented. A true sense of honor and pride was held not only by he, but for the entity he defined. With a dignified poise and integrity in his glare, we all watched on as he gave up his earthly breaths. It was a moment of true and unblemished valiance.

I decided to return back to the great market where I purchased the hog for sacrifice. I was in complete awe of the setup, as vast as it was, for I had not come by anything of the like before. As I strolled by each bit, offering goods in return for payment by way of barter or currency. I was able to purchase another strike-stone, but used the last of my money stashed away in my pack. In things true, it was just as well I had no more money, so I would not become a target to thieve. I prayed I would not become a target at all.

I wondered now what I should do. The objective in my visiting was to make sacrifice, and I did...now what was I to do?

"You there!" I heard a man shout out to me, and I turned to see him. I was taken by surprise, as my eyes had never beheld such a creature. I was frozen for just a fraction of a moment as I gazed upon him. He was taller and more handsome than any man I had ever encountered.

"Maid servant...will you come serve us? My company and I wish to be served." And he turned away, as if I should follow him. I thought how odd – this man has no idea if I belong to another and he did not even waste a moment to react, or even await my answer.

And what an immaculate fellow, so well-defined and wearing a pelt of a bear. I knew this meant he had slain the animal himself, and it only added to his allure. I followed him to where his group stayed. What was I doing, following this man - as if I was going to suddenly be his servant? How quickly I had become entranced by the stranger.

"Sir, I am not a slave. I apologize if you have confused me with another..." I said when he finally turned to me, offering up his empty drinking horn. He returned his arm back to his body, and smiled down at me with an enticing appeal.

Who was this man that suddenly caused my stomach to flutter and my heart to beat rapidly? I had never experienced one as him, or feelings as these, before in my life. Suddenly I remembered Thorfinn, and realized how very vulnerable I had just allowed myself to become. Without speaking another word, I back-stepped away from the man and his crowd.

"Woman – wait!" I heard his voice again.

"I requested that you *stop!*" I pretended to not notice him too much as I stopped to oblige, allowing him to catch up to me.

"What is your name?" he asked

"What is *your* name, I should ask?"

"Stormi. I and my family are here for the celebrations, of course." He answered.

"Stormi!" A man called out to him, to which he attended and returned to his group. I was unsure if he assumed I would remain and wait there for him, but I left immediately. I wished to return to my makeshift shelter before dark.

I passed by the slaves, all sporadically strewn about wherever they could find comfort. Some were for sale, foreigners from distant raids, while others were just thralls. I listened in as one of them told the others he had received freedom on his way to the festivals. He promised to still be of assistance to his former owner while in Uppsala, but was promised he would do this as a free man. Now he was attempting to sell some of his clothing. The man justified his intention to earn and save enough money to buy his way out of any further celebrations. He explained it was all in order to change his faith to that of a 'Christian.'

"As Christians, we are *all* created *in* a god's image...we are *as* gods, and slave to none..!" He went further to educate the others.

What was this belief, *Christian*? I had never heard of such a thing, and found myself eavesdropping to hear if he might reveal the meaning of it. As I let my guard down in curiosity, I was suddenly rushed into by a large and rancid smelling man.

"You have no one to belong to, do you maid?" The man laughed as he spit into my ear.

"Let go of me..!" I warned him, as he gripped my rear with one hand and squeezed my arm with the other.

"I watched you very early this morning. What did you do? Did you murder your owner in transit here? I will own you then."

I slammed into his throat with the stiff edge of my palm. I wanted him to know I was serious when I *ordered* he release me.

"Your affections are unwanted! Quit, do not ambush me!" I yelled in threat, as I saw the man dash back at me, landing onto the ground as intensely as his blow to my side. I had never been struck so hard, and I rose to my feet quickly in order to show I was without fear. I went for my wand and held it out to show him as I warned him.

"I am a seiðkona, and I will do *anything* to protect myself!" I cautioned him, while swiftly taking up my axe in my other hand. In an instant, I prepared my mind for bloodshed.

He suddenly looked unsure, raising his hands in surrender, and all-at-once stopped coming at me. There was a moment of peace, since he was now alarmed. He swallowed in uneasiness as sweat began to bead below his hairline. He was very wise to resist any further action against me, as all were aware of the powers held by a völva, including her potential for harming another. I was not one to abuse the powers in my abilities - but I *would* defend myself. I knew this man was aware of his mistake, and I allowed him to leave where I stayed.

"Yes, leave me, and next time you should not be so sure of another's aim or situation *before* deciding to take a matter into your own hands! Now *GO* away from me!" He did as I demanded, and I felt relief knowing I could be protected by my wand, as well as my weapon.

Feeling all the more fatigued, I turned back toward my shelter, when suddenly the thunder of a man's scream ripped through the atmosphere, shutting down everyone and every thing's movement. I followed a crowd of people, all of us running to where the howl originated.

The cry came from within the temple. Upon entering, we all saw a woman hanging by her twisted neck from the shrine. Her body moved back and forth and with a morbid expression upon her face.

"Someone...please help me cut her down...oh, mother - why did you do this?" The young man was the one who had yelled, alerting everyone. He said to be the woman's son, and he finally received assistance in cutting her down. As they carried her body away, her half-opened eyes passed by mine. Although it was brief, it was also a long enough moment for images *of* her to flash in my mind... and then, to my surprise, I actually *saw* how this had happened to her.

...The woman had been alive, about an hour's time before. She had discovered the bloody and murdered frame of her father, to which she became ravaged in grief and mourning. A small portion of time later, her husband entered the tent with blood covering his hands and garments.

"*Heiðrekr*!" Addressing her husband by his name, she became infuriated.

"What is it you have done...*what* have you DONE?!" She picked up a small log of wood, throwing it at him. Then she left their shelter, carrying herself into the temple and up to the shrine for her final moment. I *saw* all of these things, as they acted out in my mind.

"How awful," I thought aloud. Disgusted, I moved on back to my temporary dwelling to see it had remained untouched. I was pleasantly surprised to find it had, and chose to settle back in to my spot between the two evergreens. I noticed Boulder now to be untied, but thankfully still remained near.

Removing my new strike-stone, I prepared my fire. Within moments, I was warm. My eyes grew heavy and I struggled to keep them open. So much fresh air certainly tired me enough. Curiously, I found I was more tired than hungry, resolving not to eat until the following day. I finally allowed my eyes to surrender their fight to remain open, and I slept.

CHAPTER EIGHT

Frideberg's Daughter

I awoke safely to another day. It finally arrived upon the day in the festivities when the Thing of All Swedes was to take place. We held Thing events in large, open spaces. Runes were shaved into pieces of bark, and they served as the answers from the gods. A question was asked, then a piece of bark was thrown onto a sheet. Whatever the runic message displayed was the disposition of the gods, and was known to us as the act of *casting lots*. The will of the people would be heard by the King, and great decisions would be made – decisions effecting us forevermore.   This was the most important of assemblies, and the most powerful man in attendance was not even King Bjorn himself; rather the one called the '*lawspeaker of Tiundaland*,' - it was he whom all awaited to hear the final word spoken.

There was already a Thing taking place, deciding whether or not to make a marital union official. The idea of it brought me back to the day Helgi mentioned it to Hendrik not too long before, as we all stood in the hall of my home. How I missed father, Helgi and the farm.

Now, these two rival clans were settling their pasts, calling a truce. I stood in the distance, over-hearing a random word here and there. Then I noticed the name of the man who was to marry the young woman.

"...Stormi Bjornsson," My eyes could not help themselves as they intently looked to see the man who was being referred to. To my surprise, there he stood – the same man who had approached me the previous day near the market. With his confident glare, he embodied warrior strength. I could see the sword he held at his side and the signature name engraved near the handle - it was a famed *Ulfberht s*word, brandished by only the wealthiest of warriors. Its blade was known to be most resilient and best of its kind.

Indeed, I was not surprised Stormi owned such a prized possession, as he was example to all things larger than life. Others admired him as well, and his smile was one that could win over the grittiest of demeanors. He truly looked as a bear: strong, respected and magnificent.

I forced my eyes to look away from him, as I likely could have for the remainder of the day. I was quickly distracted when a man spit on the ground and spoke up angrily at the idea of unity.

"I would not wife my mangiest bitch to their fattest swine, let alone my sister, here...*even* if it meant we would be clans who find 'peace'! They are *filthy*, the Bjornssons!" One spoke up with harsh words. I chuckled, since there was irony in the moment: This man now accused Stormi and his kin to be less refined, when the crowd here held witness to his ill meaning declaration. As another spoke to him, I learned of his name.

"Resist speaking these ill words, Muerich – leave it!" I could surmise it was his father who urged him under his breath, in hopes no one would hear.

"Ha! I must ask, then Muerich. How filthy would I be standing a hand's distance to you with my blade at your throat? Do you think I have dirt in my fingernails?" Shouting a question was a man likely to be Stormi's brother. From the whispers in the crowd around me, I learned his name was 'Geir.' He, Stormi and the rest of these men were well-known Swede Vikings and warriors.

No one said a word, and tension grew thick in the field we all now awkwardly stood in.

"I would *most* enjoy ..." Geir smiled as he continued his threat, "giving you such an opportunity to investigate the *extent* of my filth... " He fearlessly tuned out the glares from the men in Muerich's crowd. Boldly, Geir fixated the promising smirk at him.

"Let us see, Geir!" a random voice provoked.

"Yes! Come at us and we can seek the answer for you!" another man called out.

"No – this is the union we seek, here, today!" Reasoned an uncle of Stormi and Geir.

Suddenly, Muerich pulled his sword and charged at Geir. Stormi raised his Ulfberht, waiting the perfect moment to *strike* it down, and as brutally as he could.

Within a moment's notice, everything oddly ceased as a cloak was thrown onto Muerich by his mother. His cousin and Stormi's sisters threw more garments at the men. Stormi's sister held onto a long walking stick, and pushed it at the men to divide them. While they became preoccupied removing the fabric from their blades and repositioning their stances, all seriousness soon became lost.

Who could not laugh at each foolish yet fierce warrior, as he snarled while covered in a maiden's cloak? All did but Muerich, who pretended to ease. The murderous expression pulsating in his stare said otherwise. My eyes caught sight of Stormi, once more, and it was difficult to pull them away from his form. I then turned to watch Muerich as he exited the field. He walked toward the direction I stood and I was unnoticed as Muerich passed by me, his shoulder burying itself into mine.

"Move away from the path I walk, woman! Did you not see me?" He asked me, speaking venomously. He shocked me with his foul tongue.

"Actually no, I hadn't - as I do not see *anything* to notice." I looked at him from top to bottom, showing fear was not sparked within me when he spoke. I was not one to scare easily by men less worthy than Helgi or Thorfinn.

The obvious lack of manners in this man made him appear puny and weak, and I *saw* the insecurity and small intelligence this man embodied. It was difficult for me to find him anything but shameful and ridiculous. I could *see* how much he envied Stormi – that was the true motivation behind his hatred. Stormi was exactly everything this failure of an honorable man, Muerich was *not*.

Behind me, much noise was being made from some chieftains, the men who oversaw the surrounding regions. The majority of the men spoke out they were...

"..opposed! I do not support this man Ansgar!" One chieftain barked.

"I agree! What will the Christian laws do to us? How could we ever compromise?" Another probed.

"Men…! We will cast the lots then, to see what the gods say of this merging. I believe they will show they approve! " Announced King Bjorn, obviously irritated with their opposition.

"In the field we shall throw the lots, and then the gods will decide." He shouted.

I was still able to hear the men spouting at each other, and with more steam than an oven. The lots were tossed, and the decision was made.

"It is now known - we will accept Christianity and this priest Ansgar."

Some were in shock as an absence of sound blanketed all witnessing the significant announcement. The moment lasted but a fraction of time before a voice was heard.

"This is unwise!"   An elderly man hollered from the middle of the crowd.

"What now happens to our gods…?"

"Will we be cast out from our homes then, if we choose not to know it?   May we decide?"

"It is *very* wise and listen…listen to me! I will tell you why!" Muerich pleaded with the small crowd to be heard.

"All of us who must regularly travel to the Frisian town of Dorestad to trade - you *know* what I speak of…! If we were to accept their god as ours, we will be allowed to continue our way without taking any effort to draw our blades. We will not be stopped or questioned - or even threatened. Ignore the old men and women. It is their god, 'Christ' we must also now worship, and let into our tradition!"

The herald corralled the chieftains, waving his arms, and each man directed their complaints with him. Everyone fell silent except the King as he shouted,

"I wish to see Stormi Bjornsson and Muerich Jegersson - bring them to me!"

Both men were in distance enough to hear the King call out their name, and I watched as Stormi immediately went to the King. Muerich however, boldly remained back and approached me. He then had the audacity to ask whom it was I belonged to.

I straightened my back and lifted my chin, as there was honor in my name, and I was proud to declare.

"My name is Mist and I am a völva. I belong to no man but my father, Thorfinn. My mother is Hilde, and I am come from Eida-Skog, Norway."

Muerich did not speak or ask anything more of me. His color changed, and confusion danced in his glare. As Muerich turned to walk away from me, it was disturbing the way a smile formed on his lips. I began to walk away, but what my ears heard next caused me to run *after* him.

"Ah yes – Hilde Hedvinsdotter..!"

Not many would know of mother's name, and for some reason, this man did. I needed to learn what he may know of Hilde.

I came as close as I was permitted to, then remained a respectful distance from the men and King Bjorn. He pointed toward Muerich and Stormi, directing each man to follow him.

The King led Stormi and Muerich far enough away so that no one may hear them. I closed my eyes and imagined myself wandering up right in the middle of them all. Just as when Egil and my father spoke in our hall, I was able to hear *everything* said between the King, Stormi, and Muerich.

"What is it you two bicker about, *now*?" the King began with a question. Stormi and Muerich remained quiet, in respect.

"You both bleed the same color red, and are two of my best warriors! Do not act as a petty house-maid and quarrel over the natural progression of your families' fate! Muerich – unless you wish to upset *my* plans and *my orders,* I suggest you do not wage combat with Stormi *again!"* The King's eyes were held wide open, and Muerich understood.

"Do you also agree, Stormi? I am the King, and my orders over-rule your family disputes." The King turned now to point his finger directly at Muerich as he continued.

"…and Muerich - you will be renounced and dishonored without breathing another day if only a *rumor* of such behavior is found in you again. Be warned: it had *best* remain a safe distance from my ear!

"You both are aware of the backlashes made against me and this Christian priest, Ansgar. When it was proposed he build a Christian temple in Bjorko, things did not go over well with the people there. I think we *should* let him build it. Such a maneuver will permit the best leverage for trade with our Christian neighbors." The King a deep breath in angst, the King continued to explain his case. "…Besides, I do not want any unwanted attention from Louis the Pious."

"Yes Bjorn, I understand." Stormi promised.

"I, too, understand; but I do not trust this man becau-," Muerich could not resist an opportunity to insult Stormi, and King Bjorn stepped right in.

"No MORE, Muerich – enough! Need I remind you of Charlemagne? King Horik of Denmark has already led by example, and now has even opened trade within those lands. I will need you - *both* of you - to help protect the transition, as it must carry on without any more upheaval! That is all. Go on as you were, and remember my warning."

Stormi and Muerich looked briefly at one another, then began to leave the area with their King.

"Oh..! Men, wait – I almost forgot to mention the first order of interest, requested by the Christian Ansgar." He waited for Stormi and Muerich to return to him.

"He has a concern, Ansgar and his helper Witmar - they express worry for the safe delivery of a young woman 'Catla.' She is the only daughter belonging to the woman Friedberg, a Christian convert who recently died. Catla must return to Dorestad with all of her mother's wealth, and safely. I promised Ansgar this could be done with the assistance of *you* both. Muerich - you have accepted alliance with the Frisians and their god so well, I appoint you to act as emissary from myself to them.   Stormi - I know-"

"My beliefs remain with our tradition, my King – I will be diplomatic for the sake of the land and whatever political *advancement* of all Swedes, but I will not falter my gods or goddesses."

Exhaling in subtle frustration, the King then surrendered a smile for Stormi, realizing it would be futile to even engage in debate. King Bjorn respected him, and his beliefs. He knew Stormi to be responsible and loyal.

"With that, you are to protect the interests of the mission, and of the group. You both depart in the morrow, and working *together* with the sole interest in my orders. Leave me now."

Muerich's insides were boiling, as he knew his words may not be spoken - at least not in the presence of the King. He and Stormi took separate paths away, going back to the camps of their families. I followed Muerich, as I wished to hear whatever I could. Possibly, he'd make mention of my mother again.

The following morning, I found the place where the party met – the ones travelling to Dorestad, and those guarding them. Stormi had not arrived, as of yet, and I wondered if he had been kept throughout the night by a charming young woman. Muerich's voice then pierced through my thoughts as he spoke to me.

"Hilde's daughter…*Mist*, I recall…?" He asked me, with the voice of a rat, and the look of a snake.

"You have sought me out here, have you not?" Muerich approached me, settling with his nose only a hair's space away from mine. "You have been pursuing me, since yesterday…yes? Do you think just because you are a *witch*, you then go unnoticed?" I could smell vomit on his breathe and ale on his beard, from his feasting the night before. Everything about this man repulsed me, but I knew I must color my response with some sort of flattery, in hopes he would speak to me about Hilde.

"I want to learn what you know of my mother, since I have not heard anything of her name since I left my home," It was unnerving to see how amused he became, and my gut filled with even more disgust. I did not care for this man nor his strange demeanor.

"Time does not allow…but I am sure you know all of this all ready, *prophetess!*" A few men in his company laughed at his snickering, which simply encouraged his childish behavior, and more crude language poured from his narrow lips.

"Tell   me   then,   what…am I…thinking…now?" With each word, he drew even closer to me.

"You are thinking about what my breasts look like…" he turned around satisfied with himself, but like him, I could not resist the temptation of words.

"…and you wonder if they are as soft as your mother's!" I did not move as I allowed my face to remain close to his. As his eyes changed to an expression of rage, I quickly backed up, feeling an eruption about to burst from Muerich.

"Your tongue has become a significant problem for me, Mist!" And he rushed at me with a closed fist.

"WAIT!" Stormi yelled, his thunderous voice shook the birds out of their trees. Muerich stopped immediately, looking over at Stormi.

"Pull your arm back to yourself, Muerich! You know the dishonor in striking a woman, and you are a warrior, no?!" Stormi was outraged, and it was heard in the extreme pitches of his tone as he shouted.

"Why? For this woman who practices magic? Well, she cannot be all too wise if she did not *see* all of this about to happen!" He looked around for the ones in the group to carry on with him in his typical obnoxious way, but no one laughed at his tasteless comments. I easily backed away from him, and out of his arm's reach. How would I discover anything of my mother from this man, now? He feared me, which made him dislike me – I sensed it. Like most transparent people, he was not a difficult man to interpret.

"Then I warn you, Mist - keep your distance from me, I do not trust the will of *any*

seiðkonas! She has been following me, Stormi –
since yesterday after you and I spoke with Bjorn,
until now. What sort of sorcery would *you* think
she was preparing?" Muerich attempted to have
Stormi agree with his position.

With his brow still angrily covering his
eyes, Stormi looked at me inquisitively, waiting
to hear my defense.

"Is this true? Why do you this, Völva?"
Stormi asked me cautiously, with one hand over
his sword.

"I wished to hear information - I had
hoped Muerich was abundant in. This was the
extent of my curiosity with him. I do not wish
him *or* his any malicious will. I promise this all

to be true." I stared into Stormi's eyes, allowing him to *feel* my truth.

"What news did you hope Muerich would have enlightened you to, Mist?" Stormi's breathing leveled and his sound was quieter.

"Several seasons ago, my mother was sent for…and never returned. Her name has not been spoken since I seen my family last in Eida-Skog, Norway. But yesterday at the Thing, Muerich spoke my mother's name to me. I wanted to hear what he might know, regarding her death." I told him, from my soul, and he listened to the sincerity in my words.

"What is your mothers' name?" Stormi's stare stayed fixed as he began a series of many questions, and there was a rapid back and forth between him and I.

"Hilde Hedvinsdotter." I answered.

"What King sent men to collect her?" He asked.

"King Erik Blood-Axe of Norway."

"Why was she sent for?"

"For assistance in trade, to Constantinople."

"She was killed?"

"Yes." I hoped for him to stop.

"You are of certain of her death?" He seemed unsure, now.

"Yes – this I know to be true."

235

"*How* do you know it is she?"

"Frigg."   I wondered what he could possibly ask questions of next.

"Frigg told you... is this what you have answered?"   Stormi's head tilted away, as his eyes remained set on my face.

"Yes. She told my father as I witnessed it. Frigg, the goddess." Stormi remained surprised from my words as I continued, "In her sacred wood near to my home."

He said nothing else, and took a long pause between words. I wished for him to say *anything*, as the quiet tension undid every degree of comfort.

"Ha! Do you see Stormi?" Muerich asked through an unsettling chuckle. "She is mad!"

"I believe her." Stormi decided. He then turned back to me and asked, "Was your mother Hilde - wife to Thorfinn Bondesson?"

"Yes! Do you know of my mother?" I was amazed to know I had now encountered *two* people containing some sort of knowledge of my mother! Perhaps all hope was not lost with Muerich and his stories of Hilde. Perhaps Stormi held some knowledge of her as well. I decided to find out.

"May I join your party to Dorestad?" I was not going to wait for him to answer my previous question. I wanted to take advantage of his sudden trust in me.

"Why would *you* want to go to Dorestad, Völva? It is a dangerous place to be…they do not believe in your ideas." Stormi gently challenged me.

"No, but *you* do. I will go with you, to protect our 'tradition'." Again, I felt the need to make any connection with him available. I wanted his alliance. I needed to know what happened to mother. I knew Stormi held some wisdom for me, I could *see* it in his eyes

"There is not a chance to be had for you to join us, Mist!" Muerich spoke up again, and I wished in my mind for someone to attack him. Stormi's quick words granted my wish.

"Muerich! I will permit Mist to join us. You have no say in the matter. I am to guard us, you are to act as a representative. The King will even agree, and you know of this. You shouldn't try *so* hard to make things difficult, and get on with packing up our horses and sacks!" Stormi did not even seek his rebuttal as he turned back toward his horse.

"I will not be responsible for her meat *or* her shelter – and if she dies…" Glaring at me, Muerich's tone quieted so now only I could hear him, "…then she dies." He completed his tantrum and left me where I had been sitting. I quickly rose to my feet and ran to collect Boulder and my belongings. It had come time to escort Catla back to Dorestad.

Book Two Preview

…Bringing the horses to a stand-still for only a moment, I gained sight of the stone markers hidden to the untaught eye. I observed the stones that unnaturally rose from the forest floor, and I knew we were headed in the precise location.

Nudging Boulder on I added, "All of this you know. Are you testing my limits of healing … or of my love for you?" I hoped he would allow my smile to heal, but my light-hearted remedy went unnoticed.

"Just leave me HERE! Ride on to Bjorko, Mist. You must not die today…" I ignored his request, and remained steadfast to our destination.

Upon noticing the enormous trunk of the familiar tree, I informed Stormi, "We have arrived. We must leave our weapons here, for none are permitted in this hallowed space." I dropped his shield, filling it with the remainder of the bludgeoning iron.

I dismounted, and carefully held Stormi's leg as he slid off of Gunnar. His blood stained through his breeches, and his leg would not stretch or bend. I walked him over a few steps to the shelter of the great tree, with roots larger than Gunnar's girth.   Stormi settled on my sacred sheath, and groaned quietly.   Rubbing my hands together fiercely and taking hold of my wand, I lifted them up toward the sky.   I called forth sanction from the celestial atmosphere.

A slow wind blew softly through the limbs of the vast Birch trees that surrounded us. The gust slowed, as the breeze became a whisper, and adjusting into a soft and welcoming rapture. I knew we were finally in the company of Frigg. Stormi looked at me, astonished in disbelief. He could hear her stunning tune, as hushed as it was. It merged with the wind entirely.

"Is this the first time you have been in audience of such a wondrous noise?   'Tis beautiful." He hadn't answered me, and as I knelt down to sit beside him, I noticed him gazing at me; but in such a way that I had never seen another look upon me. It was with the same amount of wonder as when he heard Frigg's soft melody, only moments before.

A meager smile found his lips as he responded, "No, you amazing woman, this is not my first bout, in attendance of one whose own beacon radiates brighter than the sun itself." His stare remained fixed into my eyes, and he reached out for my hand. It was trembling and sweaty. Yet as unstable as he was, there was a calmness about him. It asserted his valor louder than any battle cry he ever could have roared...

About the author,

Jennifer Lohr

Jen was first published when she was a sophomore in High School, and has been writing short stories ever since. The *Baltic Mist* series is her fictional novel debut. She lives in upstate New York with her husband and their four children.

www.ingramcontent.com/pod-product-compliance
Lightning Source LLC
Chambersburg PA
CBHW060548260626
47161CB00003B/1100